African Extrication a Les Retraités Novel

First published in Great

Africian Extrication a Les Retraités Novel

Britain in 2017 by XGI Publications.
ISBN: 978-0-9926841-8-1

CHAPTER ONE

...

Olivier opened his eyes and saw a woman dressed in a blue nurses uniform. He stared at her groggily and then looked round the room. His arm had a drip in it, and he couldn't see anything other than the white walls and another patient in another bed across the ward.

"Oh, you're awake," the nurse said. The woman was black and spoke English. It had been a long time since he had spoken English and his muddled mind wasn't able to form words. He struggled for a long time before finding the correct words in this language.

"Where am I? Where is my wife?" He said and tried to sit up.

The nurse pushed him back down and

put her hand round his wrist taking his pulse. She noted down the results on a clipboard which hung beside his bed. Olivier thought she had not understood his words or she was ignoring him, but she put her pen into her pocket and smiled down at him.

"You are in the hospital in Durban, South Africa. You were brought in three days ago by the captain of a fishing vessel who found you floating on the wreckage of a rubber dingy. The police are very interested in speaking to you. Mr..."

"Minetti," he said, giving his birth name for a reason he couldn't explain. "What about my wife? We were attacked by pirates."

"Your wife isn't here I'm afraid, but the police wanted to talk to you because of the gunshot wounds. They didn't know what happened to you and so are treating it suspiciously. I'll let them know you're awake, and you were attacked by pirates."

Olivier shook his head. It seemed strange he could say he'd been attacked by pirates and the nurse hadn't even blinked an eyelid. It seemed like something which could have only been said in the 17th century, but here in Africa they knew about the Somalian pirates and they were well aware that piracy was alive and well in the open ocean.

He looked himself over and saw his chest was heavily bandaged. Although he ached and it hurt when he moved he wasn't debilitated in any way. *Either the wounds weren't that bad, or they had him on a lot of pain killers. Why hadn't he been picked up by the pirates? Still, it doesn't matter. I need to know what happened to Marie.*

He sat up in the bed and pulled the IV drip from his arm and twisted his feet over the edge of the bed.

"What are you doing?" the nurse asked as she walked back into the room followed by two men in uniform. "Get back in that bed."

"I'm fine." he said.

"Mr Minetti, I'm not arguing with you, get back into the bed or I'll have you strapped down! Now I'll have to the IV put back into you." She turned to the two policemen, "You've got ten minutes to talk to him, and then I need him to rest."

One of the men laughed, the tallest of the two men, as she left the ward to fetch a doctor to put the IV back in.

"I'm glad I'm not married to her." he said.

"Well let's try to get this done before she returns OK?"

Olivier sat back on the bed and lay on the pillows. The police were his best option for finding information about his wife. He was struggling to understand the fast exchanges in English, but he was managing.

"Tell us what happened and give us your name please." said the other policeman taking out a notebook.

"My name is Olivier Pinson and I was attacked by pirates off the coast of Somalia, I was on a ship called the 'Le Fluer' with my wife and her boss."

"The nurse called you Minetti?" the tall policeman asked, obviously the sharpest of the two.

"Yes, well I was a bit muddled and I gave her my nickname. But I'm a French citizen." Olivier said slowly.

"Je parle français," the tall policeman said. "I speak French, we can continue in that language if you'd prefer."

Olivier nodded and smiled at the man. The second policeman put down his notebook with a frown, it was obvious he didn't speak French. Olivier outlined what happened to him and told the complete story up to the point where he'd cracked his head on the engine of the pirate dingy. The policeman nodded and filled in his comrade in English and the second man noted down the information into his notebook.

"We'll report this in officially and I'll send a message to your Embassy teling them you are here and ask about your wife. I wouldn't worry about your wife, if they are typical of the pirates in the area then they are after a ransom. Which means they haven't killed or hurt anyone who didn't fight back."

"That is what I'm worried about." Olivier said quietly.

The two policemen got up and walked outside the door while the short one took out his mobile phone and was speaking into it.

I saw Emile Duhon, aka, Enrico Minetti, aka my dead brother. He thought, watching the two policemen at the door. *No need to tell them that. I thought he was dead. I was rid of the bastard.*

The nurse returned and looked in but didn't come to his bed, she had a quick word with the policemen and all three moved off out of sight. With a sigh he sank back into the bed and wondering why his brother was alive, and if his wife were alive. He'd wait for the Embassy, but waiting wasn't exactly his greatest ability.

A man walked into the doorway of the ward buttoning up a white lab coat. Olivier glanced at him, then looked at him closely as he walked into the room.

There is something odd about him.

Just as this though crossed his mind; the man lifted a silenced pistol and shot the man in the bed across from Olivier. Turning and bringing the gun round towards Olivier as he strode purposefully towards him.

Olivier had moved into a squatting position on the as the man shot the other patient and as he was bringing the gun round to shoot Olivier, he leaped from the bed directly into the man's chest. Olivier grabbed the gun hand and with his other hand shoved two fingers deep into the mans left eye, gouging the eye socket.

They rolled round on the floor fighting for the gun, Olivier formed his fingers into a hook and began jerking the man's head back and forth. The gunman's body lapsed into either unconsciousness or death, Olivier couldn't tell, but he took the gun from the mans hand as a shot rang out from the door and the tiled floor exploded near Olivier's head.

Olivier rolled left and brought the silenced gun up, firing twice into the forehead of a second assassin. Olivier stood up from the floor he ran towards the door. Outside hospital staff were screaming and running away, the policemen were running back drawing guns, and third gunman was emerging from a doorway between the police and Olivier.

"What the fuck is happening here?" Olivier said to himself. He moved of the doorway in to the corridor, running and dodging right and left before bursting through a fire-door at the end of the hall. Olivier felt his sharp pains in his chest as he ran down the stairs. Above him the fire door opened again and bullets clipped the walls of the stairwell near him. More shouting and more shots fired behind him. These weren't silenced, and it was obvious the police had entered the fray. Olivier burst out of the hospital fire exit and ran bare-feet across the parking lot in a hospital gown, his ass uncovered and the gun held tightly down by his side out of sight.

Olivier dropped down behind a parked car.

Observe, assess, plan, act.

The words flowed into his mind and his military training exerted itself over his pumping blood and chest pains. He looked round, people were staring at him. He looked at the fire exit. No one was coming out of it. Sirens were going in the distance approaching the hospital. The foreign alarms sounded odd to his ears, and he didn't know if they were police or ambulance sirens. But it didn't make any difference. He wasn't the only white man in South Africa, but he was the only one half-naked and carrying a gun. He looked down at the gun in his hand. He wiped off his prints with the hospital gown and threw the gun under the car.

I don't want to be labelled as 'armed and dangerous' when the police report goes out. I want them to know I'm victim, not a target. I don't know who the two men who attacked me are, but it is a good bet they are something to do with my brother and his pirates. But I know don't want to be round here unarmed if the third gunman got away from the police.

Olivier stood and walked away from the hospital hurrying into some trees growing at the side of the parking lot. Once away from the view of the people in the parking lot; he began to run. Looking round he saw only broken fences and some people walking down the road. He tried to stay under cover but there were still people looking at him. He tried to climb up and over a fence, but raising his arms caused his wounds to protest in agony. Looking down he could see the bandages were soaked in blood. A mixture of the blood which had come from the gunman's eye and his own wounds.

He saw a house with an open fence and ducked inside the garden. He grabbed some clothes off the clothes line, running when someone inside of the house shouted. The sound of sirens was everywhere now, and he was lost in a strange city. He stopped and put on the clothes. The trousers where to big for him so he ripped up the hospital gown into strips and tied two belt loops together to keep the trousers up.

I need to be able to run.

He slipped the shirt over his head and began to walk slowly down the street and through the area. He spotted an industrial estate further down the road and moved in that direction.

There will be fewer people and possibly somewhere for me to hole up and think.

Inside the industrial area Olivier ducked behind an incoming lorry and walked inside of the fence. He slipped off behind a building and walked along it holding himself close to the wall and trying to remain invisible. He came to the end of the building, ahead of him was a tall stack of metal corrugated steel tubes used to create drainage under roads.

Sneaking over to them he climbed up, his chest in agony. He reached a tube which was above the view of most people and crawled down into the tube feet first. He lay down on the hot steel, the sun cooking the metal into a painful frying pan. But it would be dark soon and people wouldn't be looking for him in here.

He lay down and closed his eyes.

Someone is out to kill me, and I don't know who it is. I need to contact someone I can trust. I will call Cyrille, he will help me and hopefully know what has happened to Marie.

The heat from the sun and the loss of blood conspired against him. Olivier fell asleep in the hot metal tube as the city was being turned over by the police looking for him.

CHAPTER TWO

...

Emile Duhon walked down the Rue d'Enghien in Paris paused outside a small bar and took a seat. He lit a cigarette, lean back and observed the people walking up and down the street. Across the street was a boulanger selling fresh bread and the smell wafted over the road towards him making his stomach rumble.

He'd had nothing to eat since leaving Somalia in the early hours of this morning. Then he'd almost missed his connecting flight in Rome so hadn't had a chance to grab a sandwich. He didn't want to lose his seat at the window, so waved over the young woman who waited on the tables and gave her a quick order for a small pizza and a bottle of beer.

"You cannot smoke inside, Monsieur." She said pointing at the sign "Défense de Fumer" which hung on the wall behind him.

Emile nodded and pinched the lit end of the cigarette between his finger and thumb to extinguish it. He placed the butt into his pocket.

Outside the sounds of Paris permeated the air. It had been a long time since he'd returned to Europe and it was a little disconcerting the number of people and traffic. Scooters shot back and forth down the road and the sounds of sirens and horns seemed to be a constant chorus. Smoking was an intricate part of the lifestyle in the third world countries where he'd spent the last ten years. He smiled ruefully at the Défense de Fumer sign.

He saw his CIA controller walking down the street towards the boulanger where he'd been directed to meet. The young woman brought the small pizza and beer to him just as his CIA contact entered the boulanger. He waited for a moment, picked up the knife and fork and began to eat his food.

He can wait, fucking American bastard. Emile barked out a short laugh and a few heads turned to look at him. He shrugged and put his head down to eat. Pushing back from the table, he drained the rest of the beer and waved at the waitress to show he was putting the money on the table and walked out.

On the street outside of the boulanger, the CIA man was waiting his lips pressed tightly together in a thin line. Emile smiled at him and followed as the man did an abrupt turn and walked down the street to a small doorway. Unlocking the door, the man held it open while Emile entered and walked up the stairs.

"You're late." the man said. "We have been waiting three hours. I've been to that bakery six times."

"Fresh bread is good for you." Emile replied.

"Yeah, right."

The man opened the door. They entered into an office where two other men waited behind a table, drinking coffee. Both were dressed in expensive suits and both had grey hair, but one of the men had a full bushy beard. The bearded man stood and greeted Emile his hand held out.

"Emile, good to see you. How is the

infiltration going?"

Emile didn't say anything just nodded his head in the direction of the second man.

"Ah, yes," the bearded man sweep his hand back and indicated the other man. "This is Jack Cage, he is the new field director for the European area."

"I don't work in Europe." Emile said sharply. "What is he doing here?"

"I'm here, because I'm in charge." Jack Cage leaned forward as he said this and tapped the table with his knuckles.

Emile smiled and tilted his head slightly.

"D'accord, Mr Cage, Karl, Sam." Emile swept his arm out towards the table and sat down, the others following suit and sitting.

"Tell us more about Al Shabaab. We need to know if they are planning any attacks." Jack Cage leaned forward and banged his hand on the table, "Your intel has lacked anything concrete."

Emile sat back and looked at all of them, observing each one for a long time before replying. Cage was becoming visibly cross as Emile took his time, and Emile wondered with amusement if he would bang his fist on the table again. He reached into his pocket and pulled out the cigarette stub and lit it.

"I don't believe you've been briefed properly on my mission. I've been sent in by the DGSE to start a competing movement and drain resources from the Al Shabaab extremists, not to infiltrate them."

"The DGSE is the Direction Générale de la Sécurité Extérieure," the bearded man, Karl said.

"I know the name of French Military Intelligence, what I don't know is what Al Shabaab is doing, or how this man can help us." Cage replied crossly.

Emile took a deep drag on his cigarette and ignoring Cage he tapped Sam on the shoulder.

"Have you found Olivier Pinson?"

"Yes, he was at a hospital in Durban. Someone tried to assassinate him, and he escaped the hospital."

"Who the fuck cares!" Cage stood up and shouted. "We are having a conversation. I want to know about Al Shabaab. You will find out what they are doing and what attacks they are planning. The president is visiting Somalia in two weeks time and I want to know what the hell is going on. Comprenez vous?"

"I understand what you want." Emile

stood up and looked at Cage with a smile, but his eyes looked like the flat brown eyes of a shark. "Now you listen to me; I want to know where Olivier Pinson is, and who tried to kill him, and you'd better fucking find out."

Emile turned and walked towards the door ignoring the voices and shouting behind him.

Emile walked out of the office building without looking behind. He walked to the end of the street and hailed a taxi.

"Rue De Grenelle, Da Rocco restaurant," he said dropping back into the seat and looking out the window. The meeting with the CIA was an annoying diversion, but the real work would begin now with his meeting with Genevie Marcusi.

The taxi arrived outside of the restaurant and Emile paid, tipping the man well. The Da Rocco was a small Italian restaurant on the corner of the street. After the taxi disappeared, Emile took a set of keys from his pocket and moved to the small set of blue doors to the right of the restaurant. He opened to door and proceeded up the dark stairs to the second floor flat rented by

Genevie. He knocked on the door. It was opened by a stunning redheaded woman in her early forties.

"Mon cheri!" she said and pulled him inside.

Wrapping his arms round her, leading her back into the bedroom. He wasted no time removing her clothes and kissing her neck as they fell back into the bed together.

***

Later as they lay in bed smoking, Genevie flopped her arm across his chest and smiled at him. Then the interrogation started.

"What did the CIA want?"

"They have a new field director. He wants more information about the extremists, and he wants me to infiltrate them."

"He knows, of course, you can't do that without breaking your identity as a double-agent or is it triple-agent?" she laughed.

"I think it is quadruple now. I can't keep track." Emile leaned over her and stubbed out his cigarette. "They claim they didn't try to kill my brother. I went to a lot of trouble to get him on that fucking fishing boat, and paying the captain to get him into a decent hospital. Was it you? Did the DGSE try to kill him?"

She kissed his nipple before answering.

"No, but we think we know who did. It seems the identities of both you and your brother have been compromised, someone in the Mafia has gained access to the Legionnaire records."

"Merde!"

"Darling, I'm confused. You want your brother dead, and yet you save his life when you have the chance to drown him. You have him taken to a hospital and now you are concerned for him."

Emile stood up, moving through the room. He stood naked looking out of the window deep in thought. He seemed to make a decision and turned.

"My brother is a useless wimp with no backbone. Even when we were young I tried to toughen him up, I beat him black and blue, but he just continued to whimper and whine to my father. My father whipped him, but still he whined."

Genevie raised an eyebrow, but gestured for him to carry on.

"Finally, we were both sent out on a job for the family. Someone refused to pay, so my father and I took him along with us on the job. We beat the guy, but the man still refused to pay, so my father told us to kill him. Father left, and I gave my brother the gun, but he refused to shoot him. I had to do it, so I dragged the guy out the back of the restaurant and shot him in the head. Unfortunately, there was a witness, and I had to leave Italy. So I joined the legion. Later I discovered father had been killed. My brother ran away."

"So, you decided to kill him."

"Yes," he smiled and got on to the bed, putting his knee on the edge of the bed he leaned over and kissed her. "Now you know my family history."

Emile grabbed her by the throat and crushed his fingers together tight round her throat. He smiled down at her as she thrashed round making gurgling noises. He leans in and kissed her lips as he choked the life from her.

After her body went limp, he left her on the bed and dressed slowly. He didn't worry much about DNA evidence or that he would be done for murder. The DGSE would find the body of their agent, they would hush up any enquiry and the family would be told she'd died in the line of duty.

It seems we have a problem little brother. He

thought. *The Cosa Nostra doesn't forget, and they don't forgive. If they can find my brother, they can find me. I would be much better off outside the cities of Europe and away from the stomping ground of the Cosa Nostra. In Africa I'll be safer.*

He glanced over at the body before he left the room. *Strange that I'm more frightened of a gang of criminals than professional spies, but then again, spies have rules.*

Marie Pinson was thrown into a small shed with a pole in the centre leading up to the ceiling. She was locked to a chain attached to the pole and the two men who'd accompanied her stopped and laughed. She was watching them and wondering if they were going to rape her. The men spoke in Arabic to each other and then stood by the door smoking cigarettes. She wondered what had become of the others who'd been captured on the boat. She'd seen the tall European man who'd stopped the beating of her husband and had him put on-board a fishing boat. Marie knew Olivier was still alive, but of course he wouldn't know the same about her.

There had been an argument about him

between the European and his followers. They'd obviously wanted to kill Olivier who'd somehow managed to kill an entire boat full of them and destroy one boat single handedly. She'd never seen her husband in action, but knew the effectiveness of the Legionnaires. Now these pirate scum knew as well. Someone spoke to the men, and they moved out of the way to allow the European to enter the shed.

"Bonjour mon belle-seuor, I didn't know I had a sister-in-law until today." Emile switched between French and English quickly watching her reactions. He smiled at her confusion, but he'd known she understood English. "The French government are being charged two million Euro's for the safe return of you and your comrades. If they pay up then, you'll be released and returned to your husband. Otherwise, you'll be killed along with your friends."

He held up a hand as she began to speak.

"I need to travel to Paris. I have an important meeting tomorrow, but I'll leave you here in the capable hands of my men. You'll not be harmed of course. Hostages need to be returned in good form if we want to get any payments in the future. You'd be surprised how that simple fact seems to escape some people."

After he left she'd been left alone and she stared at the small plate of beans they'd left her. She looked round and listened for voices.

I'm alone, she thought, reaching into her pocket she pulled out a silver USB memory stick which her boss had pressed into her hand as the pirates attacked. She looked round the room. There wasn't really any place to hide the memory stick. She briefly considered putting the USB inside of her or her clothing. Still, regardless of what the European said she wasn't certain rape wouldn't be used against her. Near the corner of the wall, was a small brick. It had obviously been left there for a long time without being moved.

Marie crawled over to the brick and reaching out her arms as far as she could. Stretching her leg and the chain round her ankle she managed to lift the brick and slide the memory stick under it. It wasn't perfect but, it was better than nothing.

She lay back on the ground and began to sob softly, allowing her emotions to carry her away for the moment. In a little while she would stop and assess her situation and try to escape, but for the moment she was content to be a woman, not a spy.

She was worried about Olivier obviously, but she was more worried about the men who had been captured with her. Her boss was a man very high up in the intelligence service. She rubbed her eyes and began to speculate on the pirates. Somalian pirates stopped almost completely in 2013 after the intervention of various governments and their naval ships.

Was this European, and his henchmen, a new threat? Had they specifically targeted the yacht or were they just lucky enough to find the only ship with two intelligence agents on-board? That was unlikely, but why try to ransom them? There were more questions here than she had answers for, but the one thing she needed to worry about right now was escaping. If she could help the others great, but in reality it was her duty to escape.

CHAPTER THREE

...

Olivier awoke with the sensation of movement across his chest.

"Marie?" he asked in a groggy voice before his eyes came to focus. When they focused, they saw the flicking tongue of a snake only inches from his eyes. The snake was crawling along his body and had just reached his chest when he'd spoke.

The snake halted, and it's head raised up, the tongue flicking about and hissing a warning. Olivier stopped all movement and waited for the snake to calm down. After a few seconds the snake brought its head down and began to crawl forward. Its body slipped along his chest and the belly moved over his face. Olivier tried not to breath as the snake moved through the steel tube and exited into the dim light of the early morning light.

After the snake was gone, he lay there taking long deep breathes. He was lucky, the snake was a Gaboon Viper and although very poisonous it wasn't an aggressive snake. If it had been a mamba, it probably would have killed him the second he spoke.

Olivier waited until the sun was over the horizon and he took a moment to review his situation. His wounds had stopped bleeding and although the bandages were dirty, they were doing their job. He didn't know where he was other than the name of the city. He needed to contact his friend and try to get some clarification about what was happening. It would be preferable if he could somehow manage to be brought into the police station without being shot.

With that in mind he decided the thing to do would be to try to get to a telephone and make another call. Laying in the ever increasing heat of the steel tube, he mentally flipped through the list of people he could call for assistance. He decided to call his friend Cyrille Gavin who worked in Paris. He knew Cyrille's mobile number and the time difference wasn't much. Hopefully, if he could call in the next hour or two Cyrille would still be home.

Olivier climbed down the tubes and looked round. The industrial area was still closed off, and the offices were locked. He walked round the offices and tried to break in, but they were well secured with iron bars over the office windows and doors. It was obvious they'd prepared themselves for robbery.

He followed the fence perimeter and found a small hole in the chain link and lifting it up he looked for snakes before he crawled out. On the outside the road was leading back into the city, but he questioned if he should take it. Down in the other direction was a row of houses and what looked like a block of flats.

It will be easier to find a phone in a residential area.

He shrugged and set off towards the houses to see if he could convince someone to let him borrow a phone.

As he walked along the two metres high concrete wall which lined the road, he saw a red and white radio mast thrusting up and overhanging the buildings.

Olivier put his head down and gulped for air as he walked up the steep hill towards the houses and flats. The tight bandages made it hard to breathe. He stopped and leaned up against the fence to rest. Beside him a grassy triangle formed by the intersection of the road and the parking lot of the flats.

After catching his breath, Olivier started to walk on when a white lorry pulled over. It was a dual-cab lorry and inside he saw three young men looking at him.

"What you doing here Gorra Ou?" the driver asks, as the other two men pile out of the lorry moving towards Olivier, who turned to keep his back towards the concrete wall.

"I'm looking for some help."

"You aren't going to find help here, Gorra Ou. But you are going to find trouble."

The driver laughs at his own little joke, and turned off the lorry. While the other two men separated to stand to either side of Olivier. The driver reached under a tarp covering in the bed of the lorry and pulled out a long machete and smacked the side of the blade against his leg.

"You picked the wrong place to ask for help."

Olivier nodded and smiled weakly.

"I can see that I am bothering you. I will just move along."

The driver swaggered round the lorry, smiling at Olivier as he lifted the machete up pointing it straight out with the tip towards Olivier. The driver gestured towards the other two who surged forward to grab Olivier's arms.

To Olivier's left the man closest to Olivier was the first to realise they'd made a very bad mistake with this Gorra Ou.

Olivier drove his left foot hard into his kneecap and stepped into the kick onto the man's leg. The sound of the brutal crack of his kneecap as Olivier's weight moved fully on to it sounded like a whip. At the same time Olivier swung his elbow hard into the man's face and felt the crunch of his nose giving away.

The man dropped on the ground screaming and trying to hold both is node and his leg at the same time. Olivier lunged and spun to his right, throwing his foot out in a spinning back kick. He connected with the second man's jaw and knocked him backward against into the concrete wall.

The driver stunned momentarily now leaped forward with the machete, using it like a fencers foil. Olivier swept his right arm down and out, deflecting the machete away from his body, while driving his left hand forward; his fingers going straight into the driver's eye. Olivier continued his movement, travelling past the driver's body. Once again Olivier brought his foot down on the back of the drivers knee, forcing the man into a kneeling position. Olivier yanked his fingers back and across his face, the drivers eye popped out of its socket.

Olivier stood looking round, then bend down and picked up the machete which the driver had dropped. The driver had passed out on the ground blood streaming down his face, while the one with the broken leg is whimpered and stared at him. The third man was still standing with against the wall, spitting blood from his mouth.

Walking to the driver's door of the lorry Olivier climbed inside and turned the ignition. On the seat beside him lay a mobile phone. Olivier closed the door and picking up the phone, he held it for a moment.

He put the phone back on the seat and leaned out the window.

"I'd like to thank you for your assistance, and I really appreciate you loaning me this lorry. You might want to call an ambulance."

Olivier drove the lorry a couple of miles away and parked on a small dirt road and got out. He inspected his bandages. It was painful round his ribs and it looked like he'd ripped something with all the exertion. There was a small cut on his forearm where he'd deflected the machete, but the bleeding was already stopping there. Olivier needed to get the bandages cleaned and renewed, but was afraid to take them off. He didn't know what the doctors had done and if this were just regular bandages or if there was something more to it.

He pulled his shirt back down and sighed. *Just have to carry on. Nothing else to do.*

The back of the lorry was covered with a tarp and so Olivier walked round it unhooking the loops which held it down and pulled the cover back.

Inside of the lorry bed was a bunch of gardening tools and three pairs of boots.

Olivier smiled and took out the pair that looked like they would fit. He'd been two days now without shoes and his feet were a shamble.

He also found a back-pack with a change of clothes and some socks and a large ice bucket full of fresh water. After taking a long drink of the refreshing water he stripped himself down. Using the water and the old clothes he'd taken off to clean himself as best he could. He pulled back the bandages and cleaned the surrounding blood without actually removing them. It didn't seem as bad as he'd first thought although there was blood seeping from the wounds.

He dressed and returned to the cab and searched it thoroughly. Inside he found some money, a couple of notes which might buy him some food but not much else. He sat back in the drivers seat and picked at the phone. There wasn't any signal, he'd need to drive closer to town.

If I can get closer to a telephone mast, I will get a better signal, then I can call France.

He started the lorry and looked at the time on the radio. He did a quick calculation of the time difference. *I'll be able to call Cyrille in France and catch him at home if I hurry. If anyone can help, it is Cyrille.*

He drove down to the crossroads with the main road and headed back towards Durban along the coastal road. He didn't want to come in contact with those men again or the police.

I've got myself into some serious trouble now. I've stolen the lorry and beat up the locals. I'm a foreigner, there was no way the police would believe self-defence. Besides, it was their word against mine.

As he drove he kept an eye on the signal bars of the phone. When he had three bars again he pulled over into a parking lot of a small grocery store.

He looked round, there wasn't anyone here and no one seemed to be looking at him. He'd worried the friends of the three men would recognise the lorry and wonder why he was driving it. He didn't have long before he'd need new transportation.

Olivier sat impatiently and looking round as the phone rang repeatedly. It rang through to voice-mail, so he hung up and tried again. Perhaps his Cyrille was still asleep or in the shower. He didn't want to leave a message, and he didn't want to keep this phone on him. The next time the phone rang twice before it was answered.

"Bonjour?"

"Bonjour, Cyrille? Il me est Olivier."

"Olivier, êtes-vous d'accord?"

Olivier switched the phone to speaker and changed to English.

"Cyrille, I have a problem. Someone tried to kill me at the hospital in Durban, and Marie is missing. She was captured by pirates."

"I knew about Marie and you being taken to hospital. The pirates have contacted the French government and are demanding ransom money for her and the others. They say they will kill them all in a fortnight if they are not paid."

"Are they going to pay?" Olivier knew the answer, the government refused to pay ransoms to terrorists. "Tell me what they are doing."

"They aren't going to pay; you know that. But you need to rest, I'll have someone sent to the hospital to brief you."

"I'm not in the hospital now. Someone tried to kill me, three gunmen, I killed one and escaped. The police are after me. I need some help, I need to get out of here and I need to get to Marie. Can you find out where they are holding her?"

Olivier sat in the cab looking round, there were only a couple of people walking round and the shopkeeper was just opening the store now. In the distance the sound of a siren sounded and he got more nervous about sitting in this stolen lorry.

"I will do what I can. You are still in Durban?"

"Yes."

"OK, you need to see a man called Adebayo Nwosu, but he is in Bulawayo, Zimbabwe. If you can get across the border to him, he will provide you with a passport and some money. I will send the money to an account and give him the account details and the name to use. With the passport you can withdraw the money and buy what you need. Meanwhile, I'll try to find out where they are holding Marie. You'll need to get to Somalia, or perhaps Tanzania is better. We can make more arrangements from there. It will take you at least four or five days to get to Somalia from Zimbabwe."

"Do you have an address for this fellow? I will get to Zimbabwe, but it will be difficult without a passport."

Olivier memorised the address and repeated it back twice just to make sure, while he searched the car for a pencil or notepad without success.

"I'll find it. I need to go now. Merci Cyrille!"

"Bon chance."

CHAPTER FOUR

...

Marie didn't scream as the two men burst into the shed where she was being held. One held a rifle and the other some handcuffs. They seemed surprised at her calm, but they didn't speak to her, they just walked into the shed grinning. They spoke quickly to each other in a dialect she didn't understand. She thought this was when she would be raped, but one with a rifle stood back and pointed it at her, while the second man put hand cuffs on her. He cuffed her hands in front of her face rather than behind her back as she'd expected and took off the chain round her ankle leading her outside.

She quickly saw there wasn't any chance of away without being shot. Still, she tried to observe the camp as best she could in case an opportunity presented itself.

There were a couple of jeeps and a lorry parked near a warehouse which was the only large structure in the camp. Most of the camp consisted of small tents and a smattering of larger tents. There was another shed across from the one she'd been kept in and she assumed it was where her boss was being held.

As the two men pushed her along, she saw they were taking her round the other side of the warehouse. On this side of the warehouse, she saw two more permanent buildings. One was an office, a low squat building made of concrete blocks, and the other a brick built house. The house was also low and squat with a bricked fence round it. Presumably taken from the owner of the property by the pirates.

The men shoved her in through the gate of the house and one waited outside. The other, the one who'd handcuffed her rang the bell. This made Marie laugh out loud. It wasn't funny really but it was very out of the ordinary for a situation like this. In a pirate camp they rang the bell before entering.

The door opened, and Marie saw the tall

white man standing inside.

"Bonjour Marie," the white man stood back and swept his arm round. "Please step inside. I'm just having some lunch and thought you might like to eat."

"Merci," Marie said. "The room service in my hotel hasn't really been up to standard."

The man chuckled at her quip, and gestured for the guard to go. The man's French was near perfect but like her husbands she could detect a very faint Italian accent when he spoke.

Marie stepped into the house and the man closed the door and walked with her into the dining room. Inside a large woman dressed in traditional African clothing was bringing a selection of sandwiches and some coffee out into the dining room and put it on the table.

"Please, be seated," said the man.

Marie nodded her head coolly sat down at the table pulling the chair out with her handcuffed hands. She saw him look at her handcuffs but didn't offer to have them removed. Her stomach was twisting as the smell of the food and coffee entered her nostrils.

"I am sorry I can't offer anything like ham

or bacon, there is a local ban on pork products. My name is Emile by the way." Emile sat down at the table. He spoke to the woman in Arabic and then she poured some coffee for Marie and left the room.

"It seems the French governments do not have much respect or value for their citizens. I'm sorry to say they have refused to pay for either you or your boss. This causes me a little problem, since I need the money."

"It is common knowledge that governments don't pay for hostages." Marie said with a shrug and then picking up the coffee with both hands she put it to her lips and had a sip. The strong black coffee tasted almost sweet as it slipped down her throat.

"Officially yes, but I would have thought they would have more value for their spies. So I would have expected an unofficial offer."

She looked up at him and smiled. She put the cup down and picked up a slice of roast beef sandwich and took a bite. Emile sat there waiting for her to finish. While she chewed, she studied him. It was obvious he was either a fitness fanatic, or a soldier, but his eyes were the thing which kept drawing her. The dead fish eyes of a killer. She'd seen eyes like these many times but this man seemed to exude death from his very pores. It made her shiver even in this intense heat.

"I'm afraid I don't know what you mean. I'm just a citizen of France on my holidays with my husband and my boss. I am not a spy."

"Oh come now Marie, I know you are a spy, I know you work for the DGSE and your first partner was a woman named Genevie. I also know Genevie died in France yesterday."

Marie gulped and almost choked on her sandwich. She remained silent.

"I also know your husband was attacked in the hospital by three goons sent by the Cosa Nostra to kill him. You did know your husband was a Mafioso, n'est pas?"

Marie sat back and took another bite of the sandwich and purposely chewed slowly and deliberately allowing this to sink in. Olivier had never spoken of his past before the Legion, and like many legionaries had a bit of a shady past, but she thought he wasn't a criminal or a mobster.

"Oh, and just so we are very clear about what you're facing. I'm going to have my men behead you and your boss in front of some cameras we have setup in the warehouse. The only way to avoid this is to get your government to pay. Therefore, I would like to film you making an appeal to your government for your release. Perhaps you can blackmail them and say you'll reveal secrets if they don't?"

"I would be a poor spy if I were to blackmail my own government wouldn't I?" she asked, putting the sandwich down and taking a sip of coffee. "If you really believe we are spies, then why would you want to turn us over to the government? Wouldn't we be of more value to you here?"

Emile sat back in his chair and laughed, then he gulped down his espresso.

"Yes my dear you are right. You would be a poor spy if you gave out information, and neither you nor your boss are poor spies, which is why it is easier to upset the politicians."

They sat in silence eating, then Emile called the servant back and told her to bring the guards.

"I'm going to let you think a bit more about your situation. Please let me know if you change your mind. "

The guards entered the room, Emile stood

and smiled at her and she was taken away.

As she was being taken back to the shed, Marie clenched in her teeth on the small mustard spoon she'd stole from the mustard pot. She hoped the guards wouldn't talk to her, she couldn't respond.

I don't think anything will happen to me while this Emile wanted her to remain unharmed. For him to be in charge of this crew of murderers he was probably one of the most evil bastards in the world. The guards knew what would happen to them should they displease him.

The guards sat her back down on the ground in her hut and put the chain back onto her leg. Only then did they remove the handcuffs.

At least now I know the others are still alive, and they wouldn't be killed for another couple of days.

After the two guards left Marie spat the spoon out into her hands and immediately tried to press it into the padlock. She'd been chained with a basic padlock, and it was something which should be easy to pick with the right equipment.

Like all agents she'd be trained in lock

picking and most locks wouldn't last seconds if she had the correct lock picking equipment.

All I have is this spoon. She sighed and turned the round in her hands. She examined both lock and the spoon carefully.

The problem is the spoon is too thick to fit into the lock key slot. So I'll need to file down the spoon and somehow obtain a second metal bar for the second lock pick.

The first pick was used to hold down the tumbler while the second pressed inside and set the tumblers one-by-one until each of the tumblers had been depressed in the correct order.

This was going to be a pain in the ass.

She stretched out and pulled the brick closer to her. The USB memory stick was buried under the sand beneath the brick and out of sight, but she needed the brick more right now.

Working the spoon back and forth against the edge of the brick, she broke the spoon in two. She put the brick down at her feet and began to patiently file away at the side of the spoon handle against the brick. She needed to narrow the handle down to fit into the key lock.

As she sat there, she thought about what Emile had said.

It isn't unreasonable for Olivier to have been a member of the Mafia. A lot of the men in the Legion were criminals in the past, and as long as you didn't have any major crime or murder on your record then the Legion were happy to let you in. The slight Italian accent Olivier spoke with was indistinguishable to most people. But if this was all true then why would Emile tell her? What was in it for him, and what did he have to gain?

It was no surprise the government wasn't willing to pay for my boss or me, *although they might be interested in paying for the information held on that memory stick.*

She involuntarily glanced at the hidden USB as she filed the spoon handle.

Emile walked back into his small office with a cup of espresso in his hand, sipping it as he looked at the five screens on the wall. The first screen showed the overview of the camp from a camera mounted on a pole just outside of the camp.

He stood for a moment looking at the men moving around the camp. He needed to organise something to keep them engaged;

they were a well trained bunch. Although nothing like the training given to his old Legionnaire comrades.

Emile watched Marie as she was taken across the camp and the door to her shed opened. He flicked his gaze over to the bottom screen which showed the interior of her shed and watched as the men took off her handcuffs and left her. He laughed as he saw her spit out a spoon and then try it in the lock.

She is very good. Still, I will have to punish someone for this. Perhaps the cook? No, she was a good cook, and he would quickly grow sick of the rations his men were eating.

Emile watched as she began to file away on the spoon. He lifted a walkie-talkie off the table and ordered one of the men inside. After the man arrived, Emile pointed at the screen.

"You see she has stolen a spoon and plans to escape?"

Emile could almost feel the fear pouring off the man like a cold fog from a dry ice machine.

"I want you to let her keep it, let her file away with the brick and then take it from her in two days' time. That should give her just enough hope before I take her hope away."

Emile poured more coffee into his cup and took a deep breathe.

"I'm going once more to France to get more money for our operations. I want the men to up the amount of training, I suspect we'll have visitors soon. Military visitors who are well armed and well trained. I'm not sure which nationality they'll be."

The man nodded, and Emile waved him away.

"Oh, and while I'm gone, make sure to take both the woman and her boss into the warehouse and have them film an appeal to families and their government. I'll upload it when I get back."

After the man left, Emile sat down at his desk and watched Marie filing on the spoon. On another screen her boss sat with his legs crossed and eyes closed, meditating. It seemed an odd thing to do, but perhaps he had more faith in his government than Marie. If that was the case, he would indeed a silly man.

Emile sighed and then rubbed his eyes. There wasn't going to be any money out of this from the French. It was likely if he didn't keep control of the CIA the Americans would intervene with troops. He looked for a long time at the satellite phone and wanted to make a call to his real boss in Haiti. But it was too early for him to leave, he needed to destabilised and destroy a lot more before he'd be welcomed.

"Ah well," he said putting the espresso cup on the table, "No rest for the weary."

CHAPTER FIVE

...

Olivier drove the lorry into the city centre and followed the signs for the beach-front. He was looking for a hotel, hopefully one with a lot of tourists. A medium sized hotel, but which had internal parking or underground car-park. He continued to drive round the beach front until he found the hotel he wanted.

He parked across the street and sat in the lorry watching the hotel. A number of people were going in and out of the hotel and many of them appeared to be European. He was specifically looking for a man who was roughly his size and shape. After about an hour of watching he saw a man and woman leaving the hotel. The man was about his height, 1.9 meters, and looked the same shape as him, the hair was much lighter, but it wouldn't present much of a problem. He didn't know about the colour of the eyes from this distance, but he didn't have a lot of choice. He waited until they had walked down the road a little way, then started the lorry and pulled out behind them and following as they walked.

The couple stopped and walked into a café. Olivier parked across the street. It was a built-up area and there were a lot of shops nearby. Olivier jumped out and walked into a small pharmacy. He flipped through the isles and quickly found a hair colour which was lighter than his own hair. Using the money he'd taken off the three gardeners he paid for it and walked back and sat in the lorry.

After thirty minutes or so the couple emerged from the café and walked back down the road and out onto the beach. They stayed in a roped off area of the beach reserved for hotels guests. They lay down on the lounge chairs and so Olivier walked a little further down the road and sat down on a bench to keep an eye on them.

I need a car, and I need to get rid of the lorry.

What the hell are they doing sitting and staring at the beach fully dressed?

Eventually, a man came out from the hotel and met them. They had a brief discussion which Olivier couldn't hear and the couple left the beach and walked back into the hotel with the man.

Olivier followed at a discreet distance into the hotel. As he entered the reception area, Olivier moved off to the right. The couple got the key off the front desk and walked towards the lifts. Olivier walked to the lifts and when the couple used their room key to open the door he smiled and jumped into the lift behind them.

"Hi, thanks." he said and pressed the button for the top floor. The man pushed the button for the third floor and Olivier stood silently while the lift went up. The doors opened and the couple left the lift, Olivier slipped out behind them and waited by the lift while the couple made their way down the hall. They opened the door and went inside. Olivier moved to the door they had entered. Room 323.

Before going back down he reconnoitred the area, looking for exits. There was a set of doors which lead to some stairs to the staff area.

Olivier walked down the stairs and emerged into the kitchen.

"Sir you cannot be here." a man said to him in English. The man was dressed in a white coat and Olivier nodded.

"I'm sorry, I seem to have taken the wrong stairs." Olivier replied also in English. "Can you tell me how to get back to the reception?"

The man smiled and opened a door for him. They walked down a short hallway to a second door which opened up into the reception area. Olivier thanked the man and walked across reception out into the heat of the afternoon.

He walked back to the lorry and drove off to find a shopping centre. It wasn't long before he found a convenient mall like shopping centre and abandoned the lorry in a parking space. He took the sheath for the machete and put it down his back. He tied it to his chest and checked the machete would be hidden down his back. It was large and bulky, and the bulge was easily seen but he didn't have much choice.

Looking round the parking lot he found a pre-1990 Toyota, which was just what he wanted. It was the same model as the ones he and his friends used to steal back in Italy. Using the machete blade Olivier snapped the door lock. Then hammered his hands hard ten or twelve times against the steering wheel he managed to break the steering lock. He used a screwdriver he'd taken from the lorry and ramming it under the steering wheel to peel back the cover and undo the ignition wire bundle.

It was at this point most thieves would be stopped, but he'd done this many times. He'd wired the car to start the engine, but the transponder wouldn't allow the cars fuel pump to work. So he popped the bonnet and yanked out the wire leading to the windscreen wiper. He needed to bypass the transponder, and he wouldn't need the windscreen wiper. He wired the fuel pump directly to the battery. Back inside the car he touched the ignition wire to the hot wire and the car started. He took the machete out and put it under the seat, but left the sheath strapped to his body.

Olivier drove slowly out of the car park and back towards the hotel.

Olivier drove the stolen Toyota down into

the covered car park of the hotel. He didn't want the stolen car on the street. He needed to wait until the early hours of the morning. He was exhausted and put the seat back to nap for an hour.

Olivier was awoken by a tapping on the car window. It was a security guard. He leaned across the car and rolled down the passenger window.

"Oui?"

"I'm sorry sir, but you can't park here unless you are a guest."

Olivier smiled at the man, and got out of the car. He stood with the door open and his hands on the roof of the car. The guard stood up and looked at him across the car. Like most of the guards in South Africa the man was armed.

"Oh, I'm sorry. I drove down from Johannesburg this morning, but my room wasn't booked until this afternoon. So I just was taking a nap while waiting."

"Check-in is open now sir."

"Oh thank you, I'll make my way up. How do I get to reception?"

The security guard pointed to the stairs and Olivier nodded. He leaned back into the car and rolled up the passenger window.

The guard walked on and Olivier took his time making sure the doors were all unlocked, he picked up the hair die and closed the car door. He waved at the guard as he entered the stairwell.

Merde, I have hours to kill. He thought. *I doubt if the guard will look at the car again. It was only because I was sleeping in it, I was lucky he hadn't seen it was hot-wired. Foolish, I'm not thinking straight.*

He walked up the stairs to reception and walked straight over to the reception desk.

"Hello, I'm staying here tonight, and I need to check in, but I'm waiting for my wife to join me. Is there a restaurant nearby? I've had a long drive, and I'm starving."

"Yes sir, we have the hotel restaurant there," she pointed to the left, "or there is a lovely Italian restaurant across the street a lot of our guests like."

"Thank you."

Olivier smiled at her and saw the guard had come up the stairs behind him. Olivier continued to chat with the receptionist about the restaurant for a few minutes, before excusing himself.

He across the street and a quick glance behind him showed the guard speaking to the receptionist.

He entered the restaurant and sat at a table. One look at the menu showed him that the small amount of money in his pocket wouldn't pay for much here. A waitress came over to his table and smiled at him.

"What can I get you?"

"Oh, I'd like to start with a beer please. Is there a toilet I can use?"

"Sure over there," she pointed at the back of the restaurant. "Lager ok?"

"Great, thanks."

Inside of the toilets Olivier wet his hair and then using the gloves in the box, he mixed up the hair colour and rubbed it on his head. He stood impatiently for 15 minutes pacing back and forth across the small toilet. He stuck his head under the water tap and rinsed off the dye.

As he walked back to the table, he saw his beer and stood at the table. He knocked back the cold glass of beer and dropped the remainder of his money on the table. Enough for the beer and a tip for the girl.

Outside he turned left and away from the hotel towards the beach and sat on a bench until dark, only then walked back to the hotel.

He walked down into the parking lot and took the machete from under the seat and slid it into the sheath on his back.

Hope the guard has the night off, he was a little too suspicious.

Olivier walked up the stairs into reception. The receptionist had changed so he simply walked past her and opened the door to the kitchen. He walked purposefully down the hallway and then waited outside of the kitchen door.

He looked through the small pane of glass and waited until the kitchen staff weren't looking in his direction. He quickly opened the door and moved across the kitchen to the stairwell, opening the door walked up without being seen.

On the third floor he looked round to make sure nobody was about. There weren't any security cameras in the hall, so he took out the machete and knocked on the door of room 323.

"Yes?" came the man's voice from the door.

"Hello sir, room service."

Olivier put his palm up against the small peep hole in the door, but the man obviously didn't look into it because he just opened the door. Olivier shoved the man hard with his shoulder and barged into the room.

"Be quiet! You'll not be harmed if you do as I say."

The man tried to stand but Olivier put the machete against his throat and put his finger to his lips. The woman stood quivering and the man put his hands up in the air.

"Good, now let me see your passports."

Olivier took the woman downstairs to the garage and gestured for her to get into the car. He was dressed now in one of the man's suits and tie with the man's passport in the pocket. The husband was still upstairs in the room. Olivier opened the back of the car and threw in some bags with clothes.

As they pulled out of the garage, the woman began to cry.

"Don't cry, you will not be harmed," he said. He glanced at her while watching the traffic lights and moving forward. "Why don't you call your husband now and talk to him? Remember our deal, you can call him every two hours so he knows you are safe and I know he hasn't called the police."

The woman opened her handbag and

took out her phone. She dialled the number and talked to her husband. They'd had two phones which was convenient. This allowed him to get rid of the last thing he'd taken from the gardeners. He rolled down the window and threw the lorry drivers phone out the window. He'd wiped the phone before, but the police would be able to trace the numbers called. It meant they could trace his call to France.

This time however he didn't need a phone, other than hers. He was sure the man would not call the police. He'd had promised to kill the woman if he was pulled over or even saw a policeman.

The couple had sat on the bed while he looked at the man's passport. Carl Sinclair was his name. He'd memorised his name and address and ask him a few questions which a border guard might ask. He didn't anticipate any problems at the border.

The woman was still on the phone sobbing to her husband.

"OK, that is enough for now." Olivier said. Not because he wanted to be cruel but simply because he wanted to speak to the woman. After she tearfully hung up the phone, he spoke to her.

"Listen, I only need to get across the border. After I've done that I will give you the car and allow you to drive back to the South Africa border and report this all to the police."

"You're lying. I know it," she sobbed.

"Believe what you like, but I'm not going to hurt you. I only need to get across the border."

"Why?" the woman shouted at him.

"I need to find my wife." he replied, then he realised she was asking why he'd chosen them, not his motive. "I chose you because your husband is the same height and build as me. Simple, I didn't select you for any other reason."

The woman turned her head and just cried, sobbing with her head against the window.

They drove for hours this way, until eventually the woman went to sleep, exhausted by the crying. As they approached the border, he saw a lorry stop called the Gateway Lorry Stop. Parked outside was a huge backlog of lorries waiting to get over the border. Olivier was starving, and the woman hadn't eaten either. He decided to stop and get some food. He pulled over while she was sleeping. He rubbed his eyes and stretched his neck and back.

Olivier took out the man's wallet and quickly looked inside. There was a large amount of native currency, along with two American hundred dollar bills, more than enough to get some food.

Olivier opened the door and walked into the store. He picked up some bread and sandwich meat. In the back stocked with beer and bottled water was a small ice chest. He grabbed a couple of bottles of beer and two litres of water and walked to the counter. He was standing in the queue waiting to pay and looked out at the car.

The woman was gone.

"Merde!"

Olivier threw the food on to the counter and shoved people out of the way as he made his way outside. He scanned the area looking for her. She had disappeared, the door of the car still open. He walked to the car and looked inside to make sure his bag was still in the back and then slammed the passenger door shut and walked to the other side and started the car up.

Cruising the parking lot slowly he

eventually spotted her standing next to a police car. Turning the wheel slowly he turned the car round the other side of the building to avoid being seen and headed for the exit.

Merde! She reported me!

Olivier knew he wouldn't have much time to get to the border and across before the call went out. Pulling out of the lorry stop he swerved round the side of the long queue of lorries and drove on the wrong side of the road, speeding down the lane and dipping back over into the lane when another car approached.

Sweat pouring down his face with each near collision, he wiped his forehead with his sleeve. Beside him on the seat, the mobile phone began to ring. He picked up the phone and answered, driving with one hand.

"Sarah?"

"She jumped out of the car before I got across the border. She was talking to the police. I know where you live, and I know your names. You'll regret betraying me." Olivier snarled into the phone and hung up.

He had no intention of ever seeing them again, but they could spend the rest of their lives worrying, the bastards. Behind him, he heard sirens. He pulled back into the correct lane in front of another driver who was cursing and shaking his fist. Olivier ignored him and slowly drove forward towards the border guards station.

CHAPTER SIX

...

Emile arrived at Charles de Gaul airport and worked his way out of the terminal to a taxi rank.

The CIA had called him for another meeting but this time he didn't know what they wanted. Probably something to do with the militants. It seemed this new field director was a bit obsessed with the issue of militants, even though he was the European officer. It didn't make any sense to Emile.

Waiting in the taxi rank he smoked a cigarette.

Not allowed to smoke in a car. Silly rules, but what do I care. Soon I'll be either the rich or out of all this. The Russians will provide a deep cover and a home with lots of money. No difference to me. I need move quickly and it will be a couple of months before I have enough men and supplies to really cause havoc.

It amused him the French were paying for their own troubles in Africa. After he'd trained up the men they'd paid for he'd set them loose on Africa.

He flicked the ashes off the cigarette, lost in thought.

Right now, the insurgents didn't have much training and equipment required to setup a proper revolution. However, once he'd trained up a core of elite fighters and the Russians supplied the weapons it would take off.

He dropped the cigarette butt on the ground, he was next in line for a taxi. He put his bag in the seat beside him and told the driver the address.

Ten minutes later taxi stopped outside of the bar where Emile had been directed to go. It was interesting he'd been in Paris more since starting to work for the Americans than the entire time he'd spent with the French. Looking round he noticed there were a couple of vans parked nearby.

I sometimes wonder if anyone ever knocks on the window and tells them we know they are watching?

Emile smiled and waved at the van. It might not be a surveillance van, but if it was he'd certainly put the fox in the chicken coop. He chuckled as he walked into the restaurant.

Right now they won't touch me. I have the power at the moment and if I didn't return they'd have two dead spies on their hands. I'm sure they want to know what I'm doing talking to the Americans.

"Hello friend." Emile said as he sat down with Sam. "What has happened to our friend with the attitude?"

"He has been shipped back to the States." Sam grinned. "I couldn't stand the man myself, so I'm glad to see the back of him."

"Tell me about Olivier. Have you found him?" Emile said.

"No, he escaped from the hospital and then disappeared off the face of the earth. We believe he contacted someone in France. The police in South Africa found two men beaten half to death by a man fitting Olivier's description. He stole a lorry and a phone. He called a man here in Paris named Cyrille Garton."

"And..."

"Cyrille Garton works for the DGSE in the offices in Paris, and he is an ex-legionnaire who served with Olivier."

"Do you know where Olivier is now?"

"We believe he is heading north to rescue his wife."

Emile laughed, holding his sides and belly laughing so hard the other patrons of the restaurant turned to look. Finally, he took a drink of water and managed to stop laughing.

"So he is coming to me. This is perfect. I suppose I should thank the French government for refusing to pay."

The American was frowning, obviously annoyed at Emile bring attention to them both.

"Perhaps, but we need something."

Emile stopped smiling and turned his dead fish eyes towards the CIA man. Demands from the CIA would cause him problems regardless of what they were.

"Yes?"

"The woman or the boss, we aren't sure which, was carrying a memory stick with some very sensitive information we would like to have."

"To whom does this information belong?

You, the French, or someone else?"

"That isn't your problem. The memory stick is encrypted, but back in the states we have the computer systems to get us it. You just need to get the memory stick and bring it to us."

Emile nodded and pursed his lips before speaking.

"I don't believe they have anything on them. We searched them thoroughly, however we didn't look over the boat before it was sunk."

"Navy seals have searched the boat top to bottom. There isn't anything on the boat, but we've brought back up all the computer equipment we could find, and the ship itself will be salvaged within the next two days. You need to search them, body cavity searches."

Emile left the restaurant and walked to the van which he believed to be a surveillance vehicle and knocked on the window. He stopped in front of the small window on the side of the van waving and smiling.

He chuckled again, walking off down the

street, pulling his mobile phone out and making a call to his man in France to have a message passed on.

"I need the two packages opened and searched for some computer equipment," he said into the phone while waving his hand for a taxi. "Nondestructive searches, and also can you ask our client for one hundred Euro instead of the two Euro."

Emile hung up. He knew the French would have the phone tapped. The one hundred he wanted was one hundred million Euro. They would know he had the memory stick. They might not pay for the people, but he figured they'd pay for the memory stick. If the American's want it, then they will too.

He climbed into the taxi and asked for a hotel near the airport. He sat back and smiled.

Things seem to be going my way. Olivier is going to deliver himself to me and I'm going to kill his wife, then kill him. Or perhaps I'll sell him to the Mafia in exchange for forgetting about me. Yes, either way he dies.

Marie pushed the pick into the lock; it fit. She hadn't slept but worked on the lock pick constantly. The handle of the spoon she had filed down to a long, thin needle, then bent the end over into a hook to make the pick. The other end of the spoon she'd filed down into an L-shape to make the tension wrench.

A chain was locked on her right foot, so she put her left foot over the lock to keep it from moving and she could use both hands to work on it. She pressed the tension wrench into the lock and twisted the lock clockwise. The tension wrench would take the place of the turning action of the key. Holding the pick she slipped it into the top of the keyhole and felt for the individual pins.

In her head she heard the instructors voice.

You should be able to push them up and feel them spring back down when you release the pressure. Try to push each one all the way up. Identify which one is the hardest to push up. If they're all very easy to push up, turn the tension wrench more to increase the torque. If one won't go up at all, ease the torque until you can push it up.

She felt along until she found a stubborn pin. She pressed the stubborn pin with just enough pressure to overcome the downward pressure of the spring.

Remember, the pin is actually a pair of pins. Your pick is pushing against the lower pin, which in turn pushes against the upper pin. Your goal is to push the upper pin completely out of the cylinder.

He'd stood over her at that point and held her hands to show her how to do it properly.

When you stop pushing, the lower pin will fall back down into the cylinder. However, the torque on the cylinder will result in a misalignment of the hole. In the cylinder, with the hole in the housing, the upper pin should then rest on the cylinder without falling back down. You'll hear a faint click as the upper pin falls back down on top of the cylinder. You should also be able to push the lower pin up a little with no resistance from the spring. When this occurs, you have the upper pin "set."

She heard the first faint click inside the cylinder and moved on to the next pin working her way systematically through them until the lock finally clicked open. She had to stop herself from whopping for joy. The guards would be here soon with her food. The dawn light was coming through the cracks in the shed boards.

Picking up the brick, she walked to the

edge of the shed and retrieved the memory stick, blowing the sand out of it before putting it into her pocket. She waited beside the door and it wasn't long before she heard the guards coming.

The door opened, and she swung the brick with all her might down on the head of the guard. The man dropped to the ground, and she stepped out and slammed the brick into the face of the other man. Marie grabbed one of the guns and ran as fast as she could for the scrub-brush a few meters away.

CHAPTER SEVEN

...

Olivier sat in the car sweating profusely in the South African heat. He wasn't really sure if the heat was causing the sweat or the border guard. The road was jam packed with lorries and cars. Most of the time there would be a short burst of cars moving through and then nothing. It didn't seem to be a problem with the South African side of the border but on the other.

The road was divided by two large six foot high chain link fences and narrowed at the road point. There were two brick-built guard shacks on this side of the border and he could make out two on the other side as well. A two meter no mans land ran between the two fences, and the border guards were all armed with sub-machine guns.

The car was hot, and he was stifling in the heat. He'd rolled down all the windows. Behind him he could hear the sound of sirens faintly. He didn't know if they was because of the woman but he suspected so. There were two guards visible in the road, checking people coming across the border from Zimbabwe but there wasn't any on the South Africa side.

He looked closely at the small squat buildings and trying to see if there was a guard inside.

If the warning from the woman were to come, he thought, *it would most likely be via radio or telephone.*

The telephone would be his undoing. But the two guards didn't seem to have a radio on them. Of course he couldn't tell.

Suddenly a surge of cars moved forward and he was sitting with the nose of the car aligned with the fence. The guard held up his hand from the other side of the road to indicate that Olivier should stop and wait before moving forward. He leaned back into the car coming from the other country and ignored Olivier.

The second guard stood with his rifle ready and watched the cars approaching from both sides. Suddenly from Olivier's left a phone began to ring in the border guard office. The guard looked up for a moment and gestured for the other guard to get the phone. The man put his rifle back on his shoulder and began to move towards the building. Moving round the parked cars. The man walked in front of Olivier's car and tapped on the bonnet and nodded his head to have Olivier move on to the other side.

Olivier pulled slowly into the no mans land and sat behind two other cars as the border guards on the other side stopped at each window and were giving passports and visas. Olivier didn't have a visa, but had prepared for this by taking a significant amount of money from the couple and putting it into the passport.

"Passport and visa please." the guard said shoving his hand into the window of Olivier's car. He looked down at the ignition closely, obviously noting the lack of a key. Behind him Olivier watched the rear-view mirror closely.

"Visa also please sir." the guard said bending down to look at Olivier.

"I think you'll see it inside of the passport if you open it." Olivier said.

The man opened the passport and inside near the picture were two crisp hundred dollar bills. The man took them out and put them into his pocket.

"What his your purpose in Zimbabwe sir?" The guard looked at Olivier closely. Behind him the guard had emerged from the shack and rushed to the other side to get his partner. Suddenly they were both looking at Olivier's car and gesturing. They started across and the Zimbabwe guard tapped his hand on the top of Olivier's car.

"You can go!"

Olivier didn't wait and moved forward. The road was clear after the border and he pulled away from the border as the two sets of guards stood in the middle of the land shouting to each other.

I need to get out of this car and off the radar of the police here too. They'll begin looking for me soon. Although perhaps the Zimbabwe guard will not report my entry into the country, after all it might mean the fact he took a bribe to let me into the country would come out.

Olivier sped the car up to the max speed-limit and followed the signs for Bulawayo.

An hour out of the city Olivier pulled off to the side of the road and ditched the car.

He removed the back pack from the car and looked at the machete. Although it would be useful to have the weapon, it wouldn't be a good idea to wander through the country on a stolen passport carrying a noticeable weapon. He threw the machete back into the car and took the screw driver out of the ignition.

It will do.

"Hello, are you Adebayo Nwosu?" Olivier asked standing on the porch of a small house. The man looking at him was very tall with a small beard, tightly shaven close to his skin. The hair was full and bushy.

"Yes, who are you?"

"Je'm appele Olivier Piston," Olivier switched to French. He spoke French in order to ensure the man spoke fluently and let him know Olivier was the person who was supposed to meet him.

"Bonjour, entre," the man replied and invited him into the house with a gesture.

The inside of the house was nice and tidy

with nothing to indicate the mans work. He looked at Olivier and asked him the name of the person who sent him. Happy with Olivier's reply he took him out the back of the house to a small kitchen and offered him a coffee.

Olivier stood sipping the strong black espresso while the man took a box out from under the kitchen sink and opened the lock.

"I have a French passport for you. It has all the official fixings, except the computer chip used to store your biometric information is blank." The man handed over the passport. "Your friend emailed me a photograph, and I used it to put into the passport. The biometric chip isn't a problem you'll encounter when travelling outside of Europe. None of the countries in Africa are using it, so it will not be scanned and you'll not be questioned.

Olivier examined the passport closely; it was perfect and wouldn't be commented on even in Paris. It was made out in the name of Henry Pettre.

Il est parfait!

He smiled and nodded to the man who was pouring himself a coffee and sitting down at the table.

"Are you hungry?" the man asked, "I have some beans cooking."

Olivier looked at the pot of bubbling beans but shook his head no, even though he was actually hungry. He would eat later.

"No, what about the money?"

The man smiled and pulled a small bank book from the box.

"I had my friend at the bank open the account yesterday using those passport details. it will not be a problem for you to access it. Your friend has transferred money into the account, although I don't know how much. You can just head over to the Barclays bank on this street and make a withdraw."

Olivier nodded and put the bankbook and the passport into his pocket.

"Thank you, can I leave my backpack here? I want to call my friend in Paris after I get the money if that is OK? I will, of course, pay for the phone charges."

The man nodded and stood showing Olivier to the door. As Olivier walked out on to the porch, the man up his hand on his shoulder.

"Be careful when you come out of the bank, there are thieves who wait to rob people coming from the bank. Get your money and come directly back here."

"Sure."

Olivier walked down the street which looked like just about every other African street he'd seen. It was paved, but the potholes were deep and the majority of the street was more dirt than pavement. The bank sat off the side of the street on a small corner lot. It was clean and air-conditioned for which he was very grateful. He waited patiently in the queue and putting the bankbook and his passport under the glass when he got to the window. He asked if he could get a balance on the account and withdraw some money.

"Certainly sir." the man behind the counter said. He checked the account quickly in his computer terminal and then looked at Olivier.

"You have an account balance of ten thousand US dollars, however you can only withdraw round five hundred dollars at this branch each day."

Olivier was surprised to find so much money, he wasn't really sure how Cyrille had managed to come up with it. Still, he wasn't going to argue.

"That will be fine, I'll take the five hundred in local currency, and one hundred in US dollars now. I assume I can withdraw at any branch? I plan to do some travelling round the country and I wanted to have money on hand."

"Certainly sir, you can withdraw at any branch worldwide."

Olivier nodded and took the cash and waited while the bankbook was updated and stamped.

He worried about pick-pockets, so stuffed the money down into his underwear before leaving the building. The security guard watched him and nodded with approval.

Outside Olivier walked back towards Adeboayo's house and kept his hand in his pocket, where he'd stashed the screwdriver.

From a house about three or four down from Adeboayo's house four large men stepped out of the door and walked towards Olivier. It wasn't a subtle move, the men simply walked directly at him, one of them grinning and holding a baseball bat.

"OK, give us the money Frenchman."

He looked at the man and laughed. It seemed Adebayo was right, men were waiting to rob him.

"Oh, I don't think so. You'll have to come and take it."

Olivier slipped his right hand round the handle of the screwdriver and held it with the steel running up along his wrist. The man with the baseball bat stepped forward quickly and swung the bat. Olivier did the unexpected and stepped into the blow. Bringing up his left arm, he deflected the bat upward, the bat cracked hard on to the bones of his left forearm, and pain washed down the arm. But Olivier was prepared for the pain. At the same time as the bat hit him in the arm, he brought the screw driver up into the throat of the bat wielder.

Spinning away from the man, Olivier jerked the screwdriver out of his throat in a shower of blood and flung his arm out and round. The point of the screwdriver drove into the skull of the man who standing behind the bat wielder.

Olivier didn't bother trying to recover the screwdriver but instead ran at the third man and leaped at him with his feet chest high. Olivier slammed into the man and knocked him backwards. He hit the ground on his back and rolled. Standing up, Olivier glanced at the fourth man who was now coming into the fight. Olivier stepped forward and stamped down on the throat of the man he'd knocked down with his feet.

The fourth man took a boxing stance, bouncing forward on his toes, the man jabbed at Olivier's face. Olivier ducked and weaved away from the blow lifting his fists up in the classic boxing stance. The man continued throwing jabs at Olivier's face.

Olivier countered by kicking out with his right foot hard into the man's kneecap. The man went down on his knee. Olivier grabbed his hair and slammed his fist into the mans face repeatedly until he collapsed on the ground.

Olivier stood back collected the screwdriver and the baseball bat and looked at Adebayo's house. His left arm was hurting too badly to hold the bat, so he tucked it under his arm and walked towards the house.

"Give us the money ... Frenchman." Olivier muttered, shaking his head he went to collect his backpack.

Olivier walked to the house and stood on to the porch for a moment. He slammed his foot hard into the door lock and the wood splintered and broke. He saw Adebayo running towards the kitchen in the back. Olivier streaked down the hallway after Adebayo and saw him trying to open the back door. Olivier flew at him with a rugby tackle and slammed him against the door frame.

Adebayo tried to turn but Olivier catching a glimpse of a gun in his hand swiftly knocked the gun hand aside and holding the man's little finger and bent it backward. He kept going until he heard the finger bone crack and Adebayo screamed with the pain. The gun dropped from his hand and Olivier kicked it across the room.

"Idiot. You were well paid why would you set a trap?"

Holding Adebayo by the shirt Olivier pushed him back to the table and shoved him down on the chair.

"I owned them money, a lot of money, and they would have killed me."

"You thought I was less dangerous?" Olivier said brusquely and walked over and picked up his backpack before throwing it on the table. He didn't have much time; the dead men in the street would bring the cops very quickly.

"Do you have a car?"

Adebayo nodded, and shuffled his feet as Olivier took the box from under the sink and walked over to the man. Olivier yanked Adebayo's shirt pocket down ripping the material, and the key fell out. Olivier picked the key up off the floor and the gun. Putting the gun on the table, he opened the box and looked through swiftly.

Olivier grabbed a stack of passports which were held together with a rubber band. Also, inside were two pages of photos with his face. One of them had a picture cut out, obviously the one Adebayo had used for his passport.

"I should kill you, but if you sit still and don't fuck with me, I'll let you live."

Adebayo nodded. Olivier looked round the room for the telephone. He picked up the gun and walked into the living room. The phone was on a small table, but the cord was almost long enough to allow him to look into the kitchen if he twisted his neck round.

He quickly dialled the number of Cyrille and waited while the phone rang he stood looking at Adebayo in his kitchen. The phone was picked up, and he heard Cyrille's voice.

"Cyrille, the passport man betrayed me and tried to rob me. I've killed a couple of thugs in self-defence, but I need to get moving now before the cops get here. I'm heading for the border. Any news?"

"They have asked for more money. But this time they are asking for the ransom of a memory stick. Your wifes boss was carrying classified information and they want to ransom it."

"So the hostages aren't any use to them now." Olivier said, his voice husky. "Has she been killed?"

"No, they are still asking for the money for the hostages, and additional money for the memory stick. But..."

"But there isn't much time." Olivier completed the sentence. "I'm moving, and I'm not going to stop until I get there, I'll try to touch base with you when I can. Thanks for the money. I owe you; I owe you more than I can repay."

"Pas d'problem."

Olivier hung up the phone and turned to go into the kitchen when he felt a cracking blow to the back of his head. Stars spun, and he fell against the table. He groped weakly for the gun, but felt a hand snatching it away from him. Turning over he looked up to see Adebayo holding the gun and pointing it at him.

CHAPTER EIGHT

...

"What do you mean she escaped? How," Emile stood inside of his office after dropping his bag on the floor he began shouting at the man standing in front of him. "When?"

"She escaped this morning before I could get inside and take the spoon off her." the man stepped back involuntarily as Emile walked forward and clenched his fingers repeatedly into fists.

"Find her, get the men out and patrolling, I want everyone out looking for her. And I want you to search the entire shed she was in, turn it over I want you to examine every square inch of it. Take it apart board by board if you have to. You are looking for a memory stick for a computer."

The man saluted, and turned to escape but Emile stopped him.

"Search the shed the others are held in. Bring the Frenchman into the warehouse for interrogation. I will speak to him myself."

Emile turned back and began to strip off his travel clothes as the man almost ran for the door. From inside of the kitchen the woman looked out and fearfully asked if he wanted anything.

"Brew me a pot of coffee and take it to the warehouse. I'm going to be there all night. Also, some sandwiches."

Swiftly, he pulled his shirt off to change. The woman looked at the collection of scars and marks on his body. His entire body was covered with scars and white marks. She turned and made her way back into the kitchen.

Across the encampment Marie's boss was dragged from the shed and three men moved inside to start the search. The man was brutally dragged across the dirty ground and into the warehouse. It didn't really matter now if he was mistreated, they knew that he wasn't going to come out of the warehouse alive.

Emile was marching across the encampment into the warehouse as well. He was now dressed in military fatigues and boots.

He threw open the door and looked on as the men chained the man to a pole in the middle of the empty warehouse. Emile walked over to the camera equipment and turned it on, checking the output on a monitor. After the man had been tied to the pole Emile sat in his chair and put his feet up on the desk. The desk and chair were the only furniture in the warehouse.

After a few minutes the woman appeared with the coffee and sandwiches. Emile nodded, and she left.

"What are you doing? The French government will avenge any injury to her citizens."

Emile didn't reply but simply sat and enjoyed the coffee and the sandwiches. He hadn't eaten again since France.

"You know, I really hate aeroplane food. It is so nice to eat a decent sandwich and have some fresh coffee don't you think?"

"What do you want?" the man said, struggling against his bonds as Emile stood up and opened a drawer. The man looked on in growing fear as Emile pulled out a blowlamp and a pair of pliers.

"I need to get some information from you regarding a computer memory stick you had in your possession when we took you from the boat. I want to know where it is."

"I don't know what you're talking about." the man said, his voice firm.

"Well then you'll have a very long day ahead."

Emile walked over to the camera and adjusted it until it was filming his face.

"Well, I guess we might as well begin," Emile smiled at the man and lit the blowtorch with his lighter.

It was a few hours later when his lieutenant knocked on the door of the warehouse and entered. Emile stopped and walked over to the camera putting it on pause.

"Yes?"

"Sir, your satellite phone has been ringing. You asked to be informed."

"Yes, fine," Emile stopped and picked up a rag and wiped his hands. He pulled a gun from the drawer of the desk and shot the bloody hostage in the head.

"Take the body out and bury it. Download the film from the computer and send it to our French friends."

"Yes, sir."

"Have the men found anything in the sheds?"

"No sir, we have dismantled both of them and looked at everything, there is nothing there."

Emile pointed at the body chained to the pole.

"He said he gave it to the woman. She must still have it. I want her found. Nobody sleeps, nobody eats, nobody does anything except search until she if found. Clear?"

"Yes sir."

Emile threw the gun down on the desk and walked out of the warehouse back to his house and picked up the ringing phone.

"Hello."

"Sam. We have located the package you wanted. Do you have our package?"

"Not yet, but I'll have it soon. Are you tracking my package? Where is it?"

"At the moment it is Zimbabwe, but moving north at a fast pace. I've been told to tell you if you want your package delivered undamaged, then you need to get our package to us by tomorrow."

"Tomorrow is impossible and you know it. Don't make unreasonable demands. I want you to track my package, and I don't want it opened until it is safely in my hands. Then I'll deliver your package."

"You're making a big mistake. You need to think about this carefully. There is a lot of weight behind this request."

"This is simple. You give me my package, and I'll deliver yours."

Emile hung up the phone and sad down on his chair looking at his computer. He typed out a quick note to his Russian controller.

I have come into possession of some top secret information which is encrypted. I want to bring it in now. I want to come in from the cold. Please let me know soonest. I don't know the nature of the information, only that both the Americans and the French want it.

Using his encryption software, he encrypted and signed the text file, then deleted the original before uploading it to an anonymous drop-box on the Internet.

He put his head in his hands and sighed deeply.

I need to find that fucking woman! Trust my brother to marry a pain in the ass.

The pain in the ass woman wasn't as far away as Emile might have thought. Marie was laying on her back looking up at the failing light of the sun. She had taken refuge in the scrub brush not far from the encampment after spending the day looking out over the land to the south. It seemed it was only miles of open ground. It would be too easy to find her, and she'd already seen a number of men and jeeps covering the area. She'd slowly made her way back towards the camp keeping in the scrub brush and under cover.

Late in the afternoon she found the stream which was gurgling off to her right. It was very small, and even a young child could jump across it, but it was enough to give her water and hope. The water seems to be very clear and probably from a deep well.

Water means life, and the stream would allow plants to grow along the stream bed. People lived near water and it was possible farther downstream she could find some help. Finally, a last desperate hope was rivers always emptied into the ocean.

With these thoughts in her mind she flipped over on to her stomach and began to crawl along the stream on her hands and knees. It was difficult work crawling for so long, but she didn't dare to walk. The scrub brush only grew up to a little over knee-height and she'd be seen. As it was she stopped and looked round frequently. On occasion she still saw jeeps and men driving over the land obviously searching for her.

She stopped for a moment to rest. Further along the stream bed opened up wider and dug down deeper into the ground.

Must be flash floods when it rains. Gouging out the stream bed like that. It is deep enough I could walk along the stream without being seen.

She stopped and dipped her hands in the stream and wiped her face and the back of her neck. The heat was beaming down on her, and she wasn't dressed for this. They'd captured her during the dinner, and she'd been dressed in casual trousers and a silk top.

They know I will need water, so they'll be checking this stream.

The top had lasted only a few minutes into her escape before it was almost shredded by the thorns of the scrub brush.

The knees of her trousers were ripped and tore; her knees were bleeding from the hard rocks and the cuts filled with salty sand. She ripped off two pieces of her shirt and washed her knees and bandaged them.

She cautiously stood and looked round. Not seeing any patrols, she crouched down and quickly made for the start of the ravine. She slipped down the sandy embankment and stood upright putting her hands on the small of her back and stretching.

No time to waste, she thought, looking up at the night sky and the moon rise. *Three-quarters full. Good, I can travel at night.*

Walking downstream she followed the meandering course of the stream bed well into the night. She was probably travelling twice the distance she would if she could simply walk straight across the sand. She couldn't risk being silhouetted against the sky, so the extra footsteps were worth it.

Marie looked up at the amazing view of the milky way as she walked. It was unbelievably beautiful with no light pollution to obscure the sky.

It was just after three in the morning; she estimated when she decided to find some shelter for the night. She didn't want to stay in the stream, so she climbed up a little and looked over the edge. The scrub brushes had disappeared, and the only thing she could see in the soft moonlight were some tall rocks. Off in the distance she could see the lights of a car or lorry moving through the night. She couldn't hear it however and knew it was a long way away.

Marie crawled out of the ravine and moved closer to the largest rock she could see. Using her hands, she dug into the soft sand and made a crevice for her to lay in. Putting her hands under her head and looking up at the sky she fell into an exhausted sleep.

CHAPTER NINE

...

Olivier sat up, slowly putting his hands over his head. Adebayo stood over him with the gun, his hands shaking. Olivier's combat training was screaming in his brain. *Get off the fucking ground, get off the ground!*

"Why did you tell them I betrayed you? I need to work you bastard. I need the money. I had to do it, don't you understand?"

"Oui, I understand, I get it. I didn't hurt you, did I? You were desperate, I get that."

Adebayo gulped. The sound of sirens was getting louder.

"You stay here until the police get here. What are you doing? Sit down!"

"You don't want the police in here.

Adebayo, think about it. They'll find the passports and the box in the kitchen."

As he said the word kitchen Olivier pointed at the kitchen with his finger. Involuntarily Adebayo shifted his eyes towards the kitchen, and Olivier made his move. Sweeping his right arm up, he knocked the gun off line and away from his body. He clutched his arm to his chest trapping Adebayo's arm and bringing his left fist hard into the man's temple.

He continued to pummel Adebayo's head and temple until the man sagged unconscious. Olivier quickly stripped him of the gun and pointed it at his head while Adebayo lay on the ground groggy and moaning.

"Merde!" Olivier spat out the curse and stepped over Adebayo into the kitchen and collected up his bag and the other items. Near the back door on a peg hung a set of keys and Olivier grabbed them and opened the door.

Outside behind the house under a wood-framed tarp covered garage was a candy blue 1966 Chevelle SS 396 muscle car. Olivier gave a long slow whistle as he looked at it. Although the blaring sirens were coming closer, he took the time to pull the pins on the bonnet to look underneath.

A V8, 396ci/360 horsepower engine, zero to sixty in less than six seconds.

He almost wept with joy as he closed the bonnet and then slipped behind the wheel, throwing the pistol into the passenger seat.

The engine fired up with the full-throated roar only a V8 could provide. He slipped the car into reverse and backed down the drive and out on to the road. Beside the bodies he'd left earlier were two police cars and a half a dozen people. Several people looked up as the Chevelle pulled out of the drive and one of the men shouted. A policeman grabbed for his revolver and Olivier punched the accelerator and jerked the wheel to the right.

The car spun throwing dust into the air and leaving patches of black marks on the pavement. The squeal of the tyres and the roar of the engine was all he could hear. He felt rather than heard the rear windows shatter as the policeman's round took out the drivers side window and exited through the passenger rear window.

Olivier kept his foot down on the pedal as the car swerved round and he flipped the wheel to the left trying to maintain control of the over-steer. Behind him in the mirror he saw one of the police cars get off the mark and a policeman running for the other car, speaking into his shoulder radio.

Olivier shot the Chevelle through the crossroads at the end of the road without slowing down or even looking right or left. He knew he needed to head towards the train-station and he'd need to ditch this car somewhere, but first he needed to get away.

I would have the most conspicuous car in the whole of Africa to try to escape with. He cursed in rapid-fire French, but as he looked in the mirror he saw the police car falling behind. Looking down at the speedometre, the needle was already touching the seventy mile an hour mark. Olivier couldn't help but grin. *Then again, it is probably one of the fastest cars in Africa too.*

From his right side he saw a huge green flash and swerved left just in time to miss a small Toyota pulling into the road. Swerving took him on to the grass verge of the road. His speed dropped and there was a loud bang from under the car. Ahead of him flashing lights appeared on the road and Olivier did a power-slide into the next side street to the left. Jerking the wheel back to the right and tapping the brakes. Behind him two police cars entered the road, and he saw buildings flashing past to the right and left.

The back window erupted in an explosion of glass as the police fired into the back of the car. Olivier snatched up the pistol in the passenger seat and pointed it out the back and pulled the trigger three times.

Click, click, click.

"Fucking empty! Adebayo, you fucking idiot!"

Olivier threw the pistol out the window and searched the road ahead of him. He could outrun the police cars, but he couldn't outrun the radio.

To the left and the right of the road were a number of smaller dirt roads. Olivier hoped he didn't have enough bad luck to choose a dead-end. He waited until he'd gone round a corner and pulled the wheel to the left on to a dirt track. Behind him a cloud of dust erupted, and he pushed on the pedal shoving it down to the floor. More red dust and dirt filled the air behind him.

Olivier slammed on the brakes and yanked the wheel full left, spinning the car one hundred and eighty degrees. Slamming down on the pedal again Olivier shot off down the road in the other direction. Ahead of him the dust was still in the air, and visibility was zero. He bit his lip. He was playing chicken in the dark.

Ahead of him a police car emerged from the dust. The other driver saw him barrelling down the road and yanked the wheel to avoid a collision. That caused the police car to go off the road. The second police car a moment later did the same thing, crashing into the drainage ditch in order to avoid the speeding Chevelle.

"EYYYYY!!!" Olivier screamed as he charged into the face of death and emerged victoriously. Back on the paved road he quickly drove the car to the north towards the train station. Ten miles away from the dirt road he saw what he wanted and pulled the Chevelle into a parking lot and abandoned it.

Grabbing his backpack, he made his way back up the road and across the street just in time to catch the bus into the city centre.

Olivier stepped off the bus at the train station and made his way to the ticket office.

There were a number of policemen standing round at the exits and he was a bit nervous but strode forward purposely and stood quietly in the queue for a ticket. He stepped up to the small window and speaks to the woman behind the counter.

"I would like a ticket to Zambia, Victoria Falls please."

"I'm sorry sir, but you can't get over the border on the train. You'll have to stop at the nearest town and make your way across the border via taxi or on foot," the woman said kindly.

"On foot? Is it close?"

"Oh yes sir, only a few minutes walk I believe, but it would be easier in a taxi, there is a taxi rank outside the station."

"Great thanks. I'll have a one-way ticket please."

"Can I see your passport please sir? I'll need to put the passport number on the ticket."

Olivier nodded and pulled out the fake passport and handed it over. The woman didn't bother to look but quickly flipped to the passport number and wrote it on the back of the ticket. After paying for the ticket he thanked the woman and walked towards the platform. His train was leaving in about 10 minutes.

"Passport and visa please." said a voice behind him. Olivier turned to see two large policemen standing behind him. "Let us see your passport and visa please."

"Oui. Pas de problème" Olivier spoke French as he handed over the French passport in hopes of reducing the number of questions he'd have to answer. The policeman looked at his passport and then at him, comparing the picture closely.

"Your visa sir? Do you have it?"

Olivier panicked for a moment before remembering the Adebayo had been very thorough and given him visas for all the countries he would have to pass through. He opened his bag and looked inside. Keeping the edge closed and only opening the bag slightly to avoid the police seeing the extra passports which he'd foolishly thrown on the top of everything else. Under the passports were the visas that had been prepared for him. He dug out the appropriate visa and passed it over with a nervous smile. He'd decided most tourists would be nervous when confronted by the police in this country.

"That will be all." the policeman said abruptly and handed the passport and visa back to Olivier. "Stay on the platform and don't leave the station until your train departs."

Olivier nodded and shoving everything back down in the bag he quickly left them behind and walked over to the platform. He stood for a few moments and then wandered up and down the platform. He was regretting not taking Adebayo up on his offer of beans earlier and hoped the train had some kind of eating carriage.

At the end of the platform was a small man with a wooden cart who seemed to be selling something, Olivier wandered over to have a look and discovered the man was selling sausages.

He bought one with the money he had and breathed a long sigh of relief when the train pulled into the station.

As he walked towards the door of the train, he saw the policemen who had questioned him had been joined by two others. Olivier couldn't be certain but one of the newcomers looked like the police which been at the scene of the fight earlier.

He quickly stepped into the nearest door

and walked towards the front of the train. The train pulled away from the station and saw that the four policemen were still standing on the platform, but one was on his radio.

You can't outrun a radio.

The words repeated inside of his head again and again.

Olivier arrived at Victoria falls train station at night and it seemed although the train did travel on across the border the woman was correct it was easier to get a taxi and take it across the border into Livingstone in Zambia. He didn't quite know why, but it seemed to be one of the strange, mysterious ways in which the African trains worked.

He walked out of the station and grabbed a taxi from the rank.

Behind him another man left the platform and quickly followed, standing in the taxi rank behind Olivier. After Olivier jumped into a taxi the man waved and a dark saloon car moved round the ranks and picked him up in the middle of the road.

The saloon followed a small distance behind Olivier's taxi.

At the border Olivier presented his visa and passport and was waved through without any problems. The taxi driver after seeing a French passport spoke to Olivier in French and explained he was from farther up north and had grown up speaking French. Olivier was happy to talk.

"What about trains going from Livingstone into Tanzania?"

"The quickest way would be to get the Tazara Line from Kapiri Mposhi into Dar es Salaam in Tanzania," said the driver flicking his eyes between the road and the mirror. "It leaves every Tuesday and Friday at 16:00 but it takes two days."

"Long trip."

"I'm a bit of a train watcher, as the English say." The driver grinned. "I've studied engineering at University of Lyon, but now I am just a taxi driver, there isn't enough work in Africa. The only construction or engineering work is being done by the Chinese and they always bring their own workers."

Olivier nodded his agreement with this sad state of affairs.

"Where can I buy a ticket for the train to Dar es Salaam?" Olivier asked. "Can you buy one at the train station in Livingstone?"

"Oh no, you have to purchase the ticket for the Tazara Train from Kipiri Mposhe and you have to book it at least one week in advance. You can't buy it on the day."

"Merde. I need to get on the train quickly. I have an appointment I cannot miss."

"I would suggest you might try to charter an aeroplane if you can afford it, because it will be impossible to get a ticket unless you steal one."

The cab driver laughed at his own joke, but Olivier smiled, he didn't think it was a bad idea, in fact it seemed like a very good idea indeed.

Behind them the saloon had pulled into the border and been turned back by the border guard. But the man inside took out his mobile phone and called someone before returning to Victoria Falls.

CHAPTER TEN

...

Marie awoke with the sun beating down on her and the sweat pouring from her body in rivers. She sat up slowly and brushed the sand from her matted hair. Nearby she heard the sound of rhythmic thumping and groggily stood and looked round. Across from her on the other side of the ravine, a woman, in traditional dress, was smacking clothes on the side of a rock and rinsing them in the stream water.

Upstream was a small village. In the darkness Marie must have walked down the ravine and through the village without seeing it. The woman stopped and looked up at her curiously.

Marie began to walk away downstream

quickly. She didn't look round again or stop, and after a few moments she began to run. She didn't know if the woman would report her or if she was far enough away from the encampment but she couldn't stop and ask questions.

It would be better to keep going.

It was only a little while later she came to a road with a concrete bridge crossing the stream. It allowed vehicles to pass over the ravine.

I can't spend time on a road. I would be too easy to pick up. Marie jogged and ran when she could, and walked when her breath was gone. She was starving and hungry and looked into the stream to see if there was anything she could eat. A lizard, or crawdad or even a rat would be a welcome feast to her. But the stream was sterile of life and she couldn't find anything to eat.

She continued to run for another hour then behind her she heard lorries on the road. This road must have been where she saw the lights from the car the night before. There was a lot of traffic now and she suspected it was the people looking for her.

The stream was now deeper and full of mud. Behind her there was a lot of dust rising from the lorries.

She ran to the edge of the river and ducked into the scrub and grass growing on the side of the bank. There were some small trees here.

I could probably find this place again if I ever needed to. Perhaps it would be best to get rid of the memory stick?

She considered for momentarily just throwing it in to the river or smashing it, but she didn't know if there were other copies; she decided to keep it.

I will hide it.

Looking round she saw a large number of rocks and a small grove of trees. She walked into the grove of trees and picked up one of the more distinctive shaped rocks and carried it back to the tree. Putting the memory stick on the ground she placed the rock on top of it.

Marie moved away from the tree and back to the edge of the river. She ran downstream as fast as she could.

I need to get away from the memory stick, if I get caught I don't want to get caught close to it. I should have left it under the bridge of the road! It would have been easier to find later. Oh well.

Behind her the lorries were splitting up,

she saw three lorries filled with men and rifles. The lead lorry branched out and began to sweep round the outside and sped up to cut her off. The second lorry moved along the bank beside her and the third behind.

They've seen me!

From the leading lorry men began to jump off the back and wait for her. She looked to the side and saw men jumping down off the second lorry as well.

Turning to the left she took a leap into the river hoping it was deep enough not to kill her and break her neck on a rock.

The men began to shout and one fired his machine gun into the air, but she didn't stop but rather began to swim harder for the other side. A couple of men began to throw their weapons to the ground and dove in to swim after her.

It is obvious they have orders not to kill me, but that isn't a reassurance, it means they know about the memory stick.

The water was a pleasant, cool temperature compared the air but it was still bathtub warm. She couldn't help but think about being grabbed by a crocodile while swimming and her stomach twisted with knots at the thought.

These men might have orders not to kill me but the wildlife certainly doesn't.

Marie reached the other side of the river and moving up the bank, she began to run, but a single shot rang out and the ground in front of her feet puffed with the strike of the bullet. She saw Emile standing up in a jeep with a rifle and scope pointed at her.

He lowered the rifle slightly and gestured for her to come to the jeep.

She stopped. Other men were coming out of the water behind her and the jeep driver pulled closer to her. With a shrug of her shoulders, she walked to the jeep and climbed into the back.

Cyrille walked into the main offices of the DGSE and made his way up to the top floor. His boss had invited him up to the top floor for the first time, and he was happy. This might be a promotion. At least he was moving up the ranks, slowly but surely. He was a little worried about the money he'd transferred into the account in Africa, but it wasn't a major problem since he had a discretionary budget of over one hundred thousand Euro per year to recruit and manage agents,

He needed to understand what was happening before it happened but at this moment he was completely at a loss for what this meeting was about. He knew there was a lot of activity and Marie had been kidnapped by pirates along with her boss. The boss was a figurehead in the business, his real function was as a spy for France into other countries in and round the middle east and India. It was on one of these missions he'd been taken.

Marie was also an agent for the DGSE, and Cyrille didn't think even Olivier knew. Only that his wife travelled frequently on business and the company she worked for was linked to the government.

The door was opened by a guard who was standing outside, armed. Cyrille wondered about this until he walked in and saw the director was at the meeting. He checked his watch but he wasn't late so he slipped into a chair at the end of the table and poured himself a glass of water. Two more men entered the room who Cyrille didn't recognise and then the director called the meeting to order.

"I first want to you to watch a video sent this morning by a man who claims to be one of our own agents."

The lights dimmed and a large mahogany panel slipped away on the wall revealing a television embedded into the wall. The screen flickered and then a man's face came into view. Everyone in the room knew who it was, they'd all worked with Luc Bouchillon before and recognised the face. Luc was looking to the left of the camera and then another man walked into the image with a blowlamp lit and placed it against Luc's elbow. The entire room cringed as Luc began to scream. The torturer began to ask questions about a USB memory stick and to his credit Luc simply spat. The video continued for some more time before the director stood up and signalled it was enough.

"This so called agent has tortured and probably killed Luc Bouchillon in cold blood. I want him found, and I want him exterminated. But first I want to know his mission and why the hell we have paid this son-of-a-bitch!"

The director slammed his hand down on the table and the assistant director explained this man, Emile, was leading a counter-force that was to organise and combat the extremists who are operating in the North Africa area.

I want him gone. I want the memory stick he was to deliver either returned or destroyed, and I want that..."

The director swept up his finger and pointed at the television screen.

"I want that man dead, removed from the planet. Clear?"

"Yes," the assistant director started, then looked round the room. "However, we don't have any operatives in the area, and we aren't going to be allowed to do any military operations without getting it ok'ed with the Americans ..."

His voice dropped off to nothing and the Directors scowled but bode well. Slowly, almost without knowing he was doing it Cyrille stood. All eyes swivelled round to look at him.

"I have a new operative in Africa who is heading to the location right now. He has combat experience and is highly competent. He can eliminate the target."

"Very good! Good initiative, what's your name?" the director said.

"Cyrille Gavin, I work in the field agent division. I can contact the man and give him orders. But because he is solo the only way I can contact him is for him to call me, or ask Les Retraités to contact him through one of their men."

The director sat back in his seat frowning, it was obvious Les Retraités wasn't a pleasant topic of conversation.

"Very, do it, but no promises to Les Retraités and no reciprocation."

"Yes sir." Cyrille said.

The director stood and the meeting broke up. As he walked to the door one of the other men approached him.

"Who is Les Retraités, is it classified?"

Cyrille smiled and shook his head.

"No they are just retired Legionnaires who have organised themselves to look after other Legionnaires worldwide."

"Why would they be of any use to us?" The man said. "Old retired men are not much use are they?"

"Do you remember the drug cartel in South America who were kidnapping tourists and surgically implanting them with drugs and using them as mules?" Cyrille stopped and looked at the man.

"Sure, they blew themselves up. Took out an entire hilltop when their drug lab blew."

"No, they kidnapped the daughter of one of the Les Retraités and the drugs ruptured inside her on a flight back to England. She died. The Les Retraités sent down a team of men to put a stop to it and get revenge for the daughter. They killed almost one hundred men and piled the bodies in the drug lab and blew the entire mountainside with explosives. I'm told the team was in and out in less than twenty minutes."

Cyrille smiled at the man, "No, they aren't just a bunch of old men."

He turned and walked through the door leaving the other man standing mouth open.

Cyrille walked to his office and shut the door. Reaching into his drawer he found a business card for a man he'd met only once after leaving the Legion. He'd spent four years in the Legion command, French soldiers were frequently in charge although technically Frenchmen weren't allowed into the legion. Things had changed in the last few years but the one thing that hadn't changed in the last two hundred years was

Les Retraités of the legion.

The organisation was simply a club, and exclusive club whose membership could only be had by men who'd served in the legion and who were invited into the ranks of Les Retraités.

Technically "The Pensioners" didn't have any authority or power, but in reality they held more power over world affairs than most diplomats. Les Retraités consisted of men from many countries just like the legion itself. And for these men their allegiance wasn't with France, but rather with the Legion.

The legion which they'd fought and trained in. The legion had become their mother, wife, lover, and the most demanding of mistresses. These were men who were harder than a coffin nail, and more deadly than a viper. After leaving the Legion two hundred years ago, some former legionnaires started business and earned money, they invested this money in other men of the legion, who also made money using contacts worldwide, their friends and former comrades in the legion.

It was still like this today. Les Retraités accepted men into its ranks, groomed them, gave them loans and support, gave them contacts at the highest level. These men controlled international businesses. Some were highly placed politicians or military leaders in France or even in the countries of their origins. This exclusive club was larger than the masons and included their members as well. A true Illuminati, but these men weren't enlightened intellectuals, they were hard men who looked after their own, men with power and influence worldwide.

Cyrille rang the number on the card. He'd been asked to call if he ever needed any assistance, he was told that he would be welcome as a member of the legion.

The phone only rang once before a gruff voice answered.

"Oui?"

"Bonjour est Gregor Whitley?"

"Oui."

"Hello, this is Cyrille Gavin. I don't know if you remember me?"

"Oui. I don't talk on phones. Come to my office. I will be here until ten tonight."

"Ah... ok." Cyrille stumbled for a moment over this unexpected request. "I will be there momentarily."

Cyrille hung up and walked out of the office and grabbed a taxi. He knew that this man had ordered him to come immediately, he wasn't fooled by the nonsense of being in the office until ten. Although the man probably wouldn't leave his office until two or three in the morning."

The offices of Les Retraités weren't anything to write home about. It was a small block of offices and flats which had been purchased a hundred years ago, and handed down through the Les Retraités.

Cyrille walked into the office and was shown straight into the offices of M. Gregor Whitley, a very tall man of Germanic origin, and though in the Legion you never really asked where people were from.

"Bonjour Cyrille! I'm glad to see you again, please sit down."

Cyrille smiled and sat at the desk across from him.

"What can I do for you Cyrille?"

"I have a favour to ask." Cyrille said, not mincing words but getting straight to the point. He'd served under this man and knew he didn't like any gravy with his information. A very direct man indeed.

"What do you need?"

"I have a man in Zambia, an ex-legionnaire who is trying to rescue his wife who was taken by some Somalian pirates, I need to get a message to him."

"That shouldn't be a problem," the man furrowed his brow and then nodded. "Yes, we have a couple of men there who can help. I'll need a name and a description and any other information you can give me."

Cyrille leaned over and gestured at a pad of paper on the desk.

"May I?"

"Certainly."

Cyrille scribbled the name Olivier was using as well as his Legionnaire name, he didn't know Olivier's birth name, but gave as much information as he could. The man glanced at the pad when he was done.

"That should be more than sufficient. What is the message."

"Tell him he has a green light to remove the person he is after and anyone else who might get in the way. He can have any assistance he needs from the government of France and have him call me soonest."

"No problem. However, I need to ask Cyrille. if you are willing to return the favour?"

"Unfortunately, my director has ordered me to not give any favours."

"Oh, I'm not asking you for anything right now, and I'm not interested in getting a favour from your organisation. I'm asking you if you would be willing to personally accept the burden. If I need to ask or my organisation needs to as a favour from you Cyrille, are you willing to return the favour?"

Cyrille sat for a few moments thinking. This would tie him to them and could present an awkward situation in the future.

"We wouldn't ever ask you for anything which would harm your country or your position within your organisation. In fact we might never ask for anything, but it gives us all comfort to know that when we give a favour, the recipient is grateful enough to agree to return it."

"Certainly, I'll be happy to return the favour someday if I can."

The man stood and walked round the table and shook Cyrille's hand.

"I'd love to go for a drink with you, but it would be best if I got right on this. Please, call me again, and we'll have that drink. Perhaps one day you'd consider coming to work for us?"

Cyrille smiled.

"Perhaps one day."

CHAPTER ELEVEN

...

Olivier awoke early when the phone alarm rang beside the bed. The taxi driver had dropped him off at a small but decent hotel near the train station and he'd slept in a comfortable bed for the first time in days. This morning he'd had a long shower and pulled out some shorts and a t-shirt to wear. He would need more clothes, the ones which he'd stolen from the man in South Africa were done for now.

Last night he'd soaked in the bath and soaked all the bandages until he could pull them off without too much pain. He wasn't in bad shape considering. The bullet holes looked red and fierce but not infected and they were healing. The worst thing was actually his left arm where the baseball bat had hit him. It was swollen and black and blue. It hurt whenever he moved it, but he didn't think the bone was broken, but possibly it was cracked. Potentially this would be worse if it was cracked along the length, but he could move it and he didn't have time to bandage it. He removed one of the pillow cases and ripped it up into bandages.

After wrapping up his wounds and eating some food, he crawled into the bed and slept like the dead. The buzzing of the phone finally managed to enter into his sleep deprived brain, and he woke up.

He walked down to reception and looked round. He paid for the room last night in advance, and so walked straight out of the door carrying his backpack. Olivier crossed the street and walked into a small cafe ordering some food and a strong coffee. He wolfed down the food and the coffee quickly. He didn't have much time before the train was scheduled to leave and he needed to purchase a ticket.

Stepping out of the cafe, he walked down the street purposefully. He didn't have a watch, but the clock in the cafe had said it was twenty minutes to the hour. He should have more than enough time to get a ticket and on the platform.

An odd feeling made him look round just as a white van pulled up beside him and two men leaped out. Crack! He felt the blow to the side of his head and slumped towards the ground.

The two men grabbed him under the arms and threw him into the van. Blinking his eyes repeatedly Olivier tried to rise, but another blow to the back of the head made him fall flat to the bottom of the van.

"Tie him up!"

"Shut the fuck up, I know what I'm doing."

Americans, Olivier thought. *What the hell are they doing?*

He tried to speak, but a harsh crack on the head with the rubber cosh made him moan instead. He could feel his hands being jerked behind his back and handcuffs being clicked on. A dirty rag was shoved into his mouth, and someone was tying up his feet. He was turned over and saw three men. The driver was a young blond man, probably only in his early twenties. The other two were older, one with a long scar down the side of his face which ran from the right eyebrow down to his mouth.

He struggled to move, thrashing back and forth, but he was well tied. He looked at the man without the scar, who was dressed in a Hawaiian shirt. This man was filling a needle with some liquid from a bottle and Olivier began to fight violently to prevent the injection.

"Hold him still goddamn it!" the Hawaiian shouted.

"Fuck this," said scar face just as Olivier felt another crack on the skull and he passed into unconsciousness.

Olivier came to consciousness with a huge burst of pain. He found himself with his hands handcuffed to a steel clothesline pole that was shaped like the letter, T. He was hanging of one edge of the T and spinning round. Beside him the three men stood smoking cigarettes and laughing.

One of the men held a battery jumper cable which was wrapped in cloth. The man took the ends of the battery charger and put it on to Olivier's nipples and laughed as he jerked and twitched.

"It is a pity we can't turn up the juice

somehow." the scar-faced man said to the blond one, who laughed.

"I'm sure Barry knows what he is doing don't you Barry?"

"Yeah, we don't want to kill him just get some answers."

"You want to give us some answers don't you little froggy?" the scar faced man said and laughed again.

"Hey, Jimbo, get us another couple of beers before it starts raining, I want to watch Barry work this guy over.

Barry, the torturer in the Hawaiian shirt, stepped up to Olivier and grinned into his face. He slapped Olivier a couple of times on the cheek, not painfully but hard enough to get his attention.

"I got a couple of questions for you, and if you answer them properly then this will all be over and we can all go inside and eat some dinner ok?"

"OK," Olivier grunted out. "Whatever you want, just let me down."

"Not likely," Barry said with a grin, "but we'll see if you're going to tell use the truth or not. First question is where did you put the memory stick when you boarded the yacht in Nice?"

Olivier looked at him confused for a moment, then realised they were asking him questions about the ship which had been hijacked by the pirates.

What do the Americans want with a French yacht, and what memory stick?

"I don't know what you are talking about. I got on the yacht with just my clothes and my passport. I didn't have anything else; we didn't even take a camera."

"Wrong answer." Barry said and stepping back applied the battery to his chest again. He held it there for a long time while the current raced up and down Olivier's body and he shouted out involuntarily.

"Let's try the question again. Where did you put the memory stick when you got on to the boat? Or did someone else have the memory stick?"

"I. Don't. Know. What. You. Are. Talking. About." Olivier pronounced each word slowly and methodically.

"Wrong answer again." Barry stepped back and Olivier expected the battery again, but Barry picked up a pair of pliers just as the blond one appeared with three beers. Barry opened the beers with the pliers, then holding his beer in one hand and the pliers in the other he clamped the pliers on to the skin just above Olivier's waist. He twisted until the skin ripped off. Olivier jerked away from the pain, swinging on the clothes line, the handcuffs digging into his wrists and blood poured down his wrists and out of the hole in his waist.

"Now let's try this question one more time. Where is the fucking memory stick, you stupid fuck."

The others laughed and drank their beers as they watched Olivier being tortured. He shook his head.

"I don't know what you are talking about, you're just going to torture me until I make up some bullshit to keep you from hurting me, but I really don't fucking know!" Olivier screamed the last words out and then began cursing them in a long stream of French.

Barry just shook his head and turned to look at scarface who was obviously the leader. Scarface just nodded and Barry put the pliers once again to Olivier's other side and twisted and ripped off a small piece of skin.

Overhead clouds were gathering and there was a long crack of thunder. The men looked up, and scarface nodded to Barry.

"Grab the battery. We'll leave him out here to think about where the fucking memory stick is. I need to call back to the HQ anyway."

Barry dropped the pliers into the wheelbarrow with the battery, downed his beer. Holding the empty beer-bottle by the neck, he hit Olivier hard in the elbow. The bottle rebounded off the bone and Olivier groaned with pain.

"You think about your fucking answer sunshine, because when I come back we're going to get serious about this shit."

The three men walked off just as the sky opened and a torrential downpour began.

Hanging from the clothesline Olivier felt the rain start in earnest, running off him like a warm shower. The rain was so hard it felt like he was being stung by a million wasps. The rain let up a little and he tossed his head round to clear his eyes. Behind him he heard a low growl. He tried to spin round to see where it is coming from, but the handcuffs wouldn't allow him to rotate round.

He managed to catch a glimpse of a large grey dog, thin, it's bones protruding out of its skin. The dog was circling him in a slow motion, moving fulling into his view and watching him closely.

"Allez! Partir! Shoo!" Olivier screamed, hoping the fear of humans would scare it away, but it was too hungry. Olivier shifted as round, tracking the dog as it moved behind him. Suddenly it flashed forward, and Olivier felt another massive pain in the back of his leg as the dog bit deep to his calf muscle.

"Merde!"

He dropped down, hanging solely from his bloody wrists and using his left foot he kicked at the dog, stomping at its head hoping to make it let go. The dog released his leg, but he felt the blood pouring down his leg and into his boot.

Olivier spun frantically trying to see where the dog was. It was behind him again. It leaped again, this time going for his neck. He stood up bringing his elbow in trying to cover his throat. The dog's teeth ripped a gouge out of his arm. The dog was at his feet and preparing to leap again for his throat.

Olivier swept his good leg forward and with great fortune connected with the dogs chest as his other leg collapsed, the dog was knocked on it side, scrambling to get back up. Hanging by his bloody wrists Olivier managed to get his good foot onto the dog's neck while it was still on it's side. Olivier stood as quickly as he could, putting all his weight on the dog's neck.

The dog thrashed below him, twisting under his boot, but Olivier stood firm until he'd choked the air out of it.

He hung for a few minutes, on his bloody wrists, gasping for air as the rain continued to pour down on him.

Olivier raised his face up towards the sky and into the pouring rain and screamed.

"Give me a fucking break will you? Merde!"

CHAPTER TWELVE

...

The CIA headquarters in Paris was a small detached business in an industrial park on the outskirts of the city. It was unremarkable in every way. The only distinguishing mark was the number of armed guards who guarded the doors. Most people in the area just assumed the company dealt in high priced goods which needed to be protected. There had been a couple of attempts at robbery, but without any success, the security was too tight and most of the time the attempts were stopped before they even started by a local gang leader who was on the payroll of the CIA, although he didn't know it.

Inside in a small meeting room sat four

men waiting for a secure connection via video conference to Washington. The connection was made, and a famous face appeared on the screen. The face of the director of national intelligence. Most people would only recognise him from the number of Senate hearings at which he'd appeared to explain the errors made by the intelligence services.

"Gentlemen, please give me a quick update of the situation."

One of the men pulled the microphone closer to him and spoke with a quick voice.

"We believe our French double-agent Emile Duhon has either been turned by someone else, or he is still working for the French. We have intercepted a number of calls back and forth to French military intelligence and we've also intercepted a phone call to Russia. However, the calls were encrypted but the NSA hasn't yet been able to give us a transcript of them."

"And this man who he wants in exchange for the memory stick?"

"We have him. Our men picked him up in Zambia and called us just before this meeting. They don't believe he knows where the memory stick is located. He was on the yacht which was taken by Emile Duhon, but was ignorant of the memory stick. He is ex-military but not intelligence."

The director shuffled some papers on his desk and picked up one and addressed the men round the table.

"I have some additional information. It seems Emile Duhon was once named Enrico Minetti and was a member of the Naples Mafia. The man you have in custody is his brother. Both of them joined the Legion after some troubles between their father and the Mafia. Both were and still are under death sentences. I find it hard to believe these two bothers aren't working together. Continue to question this man and find out everything he knows."

"Yes sir, understood."

"It would of course be better if nobody were to submit a report or complaint about our questioning, so please make sure this man doesn't raise any complaints."

"Yes sir."

The director nodded and the connection broke off. The man who'd spoken into the microphone turned to the others.

"He was very clear. Question this mobster until we find out everything he knows, the make sure nobody can ever find or identify the body."

The other men nodded and the men stood and walked out of the meeting, each picking up their paperwork and notepads and dispersing to their offices. Another day's work to be done.

Cyrille sat at his desk earlier than normal hoping for a call from Olivier. He'd been at the office most of the night and he'd told his wife not to expect him at home much over the next few weeks.

He stood beside the small window of his office which looked out over the courtyard of the DGSE building. Cyrille took a long drag on his cigarette. Smoking wasn't permitted in any building, but the smoking area was down four floors and outside on the other side of the courtyard. It was just to much hassle, so when he was desperate or at night after most of the people had gone home, Cyrille would have a quick smoke and flush the butt down the toilet across the hall.

"Your man has been captured by the Americans."

Cyrille jumped at the voice behind him

and choked on the smoke from the cigarette. Flicking the cigarette out the window, he turned to see the Director looking at him with a disapproving look.

"I've just been told by communications we've intercepted a phone call from Zambia to the CIA office in Ivry-sur-Seine. Your agent has been captured, and they are questioning him. Is he going to say anything awkward?"

"No sir. He doesn't know anything," Cyrille said thinking quickly. "He was only just recruited, and I hadn't yet contacted him. Les Retraités were still looking for him."

The director sighed and turned to leave but stopped in the doorway.

"You can tell those Les Retraités vultures we don't need them anymore, and stop smoking in the office, it is illegal."

"Yes sir."

"Oh, I've also ordered an alert with our agents in Africa. I've told them to eliminate your agent if the Americans don't do it for us. We can't know what this man has or has not said, better to be safe."

The director closed the door behind him and Cyrille sat down at his desk and put his head in his hands. He hadn't helped Olivier; he'd killed him.

"Take her to the warehouse and lock her up." Emile told his man, "I'll decide what to do with her later."

He walked into his office and sat down at the chair putting his feet up on the desk. He waved to the cook and asked for a pot of coffee.

"I need to think." he told her.

He had notification of a dropbox message, so he downloaded the file and unencrypted it.

You cannot come in from the cold. You must complete your work. We need more information about the activities of the French and Americans. In addition, you must send us a copy of the files held on the memory stick immediately so we can have our cryptographers working on it.

Emile sighed and closed his eyes. *It was not going to be a good year.* He pulled out a notepad and pushed the keyboard away from him. He always seemed to think better with paper and pencil.

"First the problems." he muttered pausing momentarily to light another cigarette. "My fucking brother."

He wrote his brother's name down first on the list and then continued to list out his problems. The Russians, the French, the Americans and finally his brother's pain in the ass wife.

I need to question the woman, but I don't want to torture her. I may get useful information or not. It is always better to have leverage. Perhaps I'll use my brother against her. I wonder if there is anyway to use him against the others as well?

Puffing on his cigarette he shook his head. The French were a problem of the past. Killing the woman and sending the video were the last straws for them. They would have issued a death warrant against him.

Silly to have been so blood thirsty, but I'd been sure the Russians would take me in, and I'd have the memory stick. The Americans will eventually find out I've have been passing on information and so they too will want me dead.

There were only bad choices. But the only two realistic options were the Russians or the Americans. The Russians had already betrayed him by not bringing him. So that left him with the Americans, if he can repair the damage, turn over the memory stick and give them information he had about the

French and the Russians it might buy his life and he could move to America. The other problem was the Mafia, which had numerous links in America and would find him there. He needed to appease them somehow. Perhaps he could give them his brother?

First things first. He needed his brother alive and here. This would give him leverage over the woman and allow him the possibility of appeasing the Cosa Nostra with him.

Emile stood and walked outside and found his lieutenant.

"I want you to treat the woman well, but keep her locked up in the warehouse and make sure she doesn't escape again. Then I want you to find five or six men who can travel to Tanzania. I want you to send them to Dar es Salaam and have them search for my brother. He will appear there sooner or later so have his description sent out to the bazaars and the taxi drivers and offer a reward of one thousand Euro to anyone who can give us information to capture him."

"Yes sir, you want him captured?"

"Yes, don't kill him, bring him to me here."

"And if we cannot capture him?"

"That option isn't available to you."

Emile walked back inside the house and the man began barking out orders behind him.

CHAPTER THIRTEEN

…

Olivier closed his eyes for a moment to clear the rain and tried again to look closely at the handcuffs and the clothesline. The pole was shaped like a T with two holes drilled in each side of the top bar. In these holes were two I-Bolts from which the clothesline was tied and ran down to a mirror image pole at the other end of the garden.

I can just pull my hands over the bar and get free if it wasn't for the clothesline strings.

He stood up as high as he could on the tips of his toes. His injured leg wasn't good, he could still feel either water or blood running into his boot. He hoped it was rain.

He jerked his hands down the pipe

dragging the handcuffs along the pipe until it stopped at the clothesline. Olivier grabbed hold of the first bit of string with both hands. Holding it tightly he allowed his full weight to come down on it. As he'd expected it broke easily, the clothesline itself was just some plastic coated string. Moving the handcuffs further down the pipe he broke the second string and then walked the handcuffs to the end of the pipe and got his hands down.

Free! But now what?

Olivier looked at the house, but he was in no shape to tangle with three men, especially as he was handcuffed. Across the garden in the fence was a gate which he quickly ran to. It was unlocked, he opened it and shut it behind him. Outside of the house he could see he was in a more rural area, but there were a few more houses up the road. A sign posted Kaonga in blue told him the name of the town, but it meant nothing to him.

Olivier ran down the road, hobbling along with his ripped calf. Above him the storm seemed to be passing and he knew he didn't have long. As soon as the storm passed, they would be back outside with their beer, and the battery ready to question him.

Ahead parked off the side of the road in front of a small house was a white van. It was one of those low enclosed car/vans used by tradesmen. There were some faded lettering on the side of the van advertising home handyman. Olivier stood next to the van peering in. Difficult to see in the poor light with the rain pouring against the window. Stooping down he looked around until he found a good-sized stone and broke the passenger window. The window spidered, and he used the stone and his hands to yank away the glass. Popping up the lock, he opened the door and sat down inside.

Can't hotwire this one. Can I get into the back?

Olivier moved the seat, but the back of the van was enclosed and he wouldn't be able to get to the tools through the cab as he'd hoped. Cursing he pulled down the visors and opened the glove-box. Searching for something that would help. Under the drivers seat he found a matchbox and when he opened it he found a spare key. Hoping it was for this van he scooted over into the drivers side. With his hands still handcuffed it was difficult to get the key into the ignition, but finally it was in and when he turned it the van started up straight away.

Olivier let out a laugh and moving his shackled hands over to the left he pulled the lever into drive and thanked whatever gods were watching over him it wasn't a manual car.

He quickly drove off leaving the house and behind. With the keys he would be able to get into the back of the van, and he hoped the tradesman was as careless with his tools as he was with his car keys.

A few minutes down the road the storm ceased and he pulled the van off down a small side road and parked behind an old abandoned barn.

Night fell on Olivier as he sat in the back of the van. The tradesman was careless and there was a bench vice mounted to the floor of the van and a hacksaw in a filled toolbox. Olivier had clamped the hacksaw blade up in the vice and sat working the handcuff chain back and forth across the hacksaw blade until the chain broke and he had free movement of his hands.

Cutting the bracelets off would be more

difficult and take a lot longer.

I'll just go and get a key from them. He thought and grinned.

Laying down in the back of the van, he pulled his leg up to look at the wound. It wasn't actually as bad as he'd feared. The dog's teeth had sunk into the skin and there was some tearing round the punctures, but it was fine. Inside of the van was also a small first aid kit. Most of the bandages had already been used.

This guy is a shit handyman, can't even stop cutting the shit out of himself. Olivier gave out a weak laugh, then yawned. *Perhaps I should start a business down here, if this loser can make money as a half-assed handyman I'll make a fortune.*

He looked for some kind of alcohol, but there was nothing. *Whatever else his problems the guy isn't a drinker.*

Olivier bandaged up his wounds as best he could and thought about going back to the American's farmhouse, but decided he needed to rest. He stretched out on the floor of the van and slept until the dawn light coming through the rear windows woke him up.

Climbing out of the van he stretched and

yawned. He did some quick callisthenics to warm himself up. He was very stiff, and it was hard to walk, stretch, or even move without some part of his body aching or firing off painful warnings.

Digging through the back of the van Olivier found a metre long steel pipe which fit comfortably in his palm. He threw it into the cab and then grabbed a razor knife and a screwdriver from the toolbox and threw them in the cab as well.

Driving the van back down the road he passed the house where it had been stolen and then drove slowly past the American farmhouse. There were no cars parked in the drive, but he couldn't see the side garden where he'd been hung up. Driving past the house he stopped the van on the side of the road and parked it.

Pocketing the key, he pushed the screwdriver into his waistband and the razor knife into his back pocket. He picked up the pipe and walked round towards the back of the house. He would come in through the back and hope they didn't have any security on the building.

He stopped outside of the fence and looked round the roof and the top of the fence for cameras but didn't see anything. Of course these days cameras were small enough to be hidden, but he would just have to take that chance.

The gate is still unlocked. Olivier slipped in through the door and moved quickly across the garden putting his back against the building he moved along to the window and looked inside.

Nothing. Better check them all.

Olivier moved to each window of the house slowly circling it, but never going past the front entrance.

Can't see anything, but I can hear music. Someone in there, but how to I get them out? Well, there is always the direct approach.

Olivier moved to the front of the house and crawled up onto the porch and combat crawled along it under the windows. He put his back to the wall and silently stood up. He knocked twice on the door with the pipe and waited.

The door opened. As soon as a crack appeared in the door Olivier lunged at it with his shoulder and knocked the door open with a bang. Standing in front of him, confused and stunned was the blond driver. The man tried to lift his gun, but Olivier brought the pipe down on his head with a merciless crack. Blondie dropped like a stone. Stooping swiftly Olivier palmed the gun in his left hand, and remembering Adebayo's empty gun he decided to keep the pipe in his right hand.

Moving quickly from room to room, he cleared the house before returning to the blond laying in the doorway. The kid was still breathing, but possibly brain damaged. Olivier shrugged and flipped him over and tied him up with some string from the curtains.

Olivier checked the gun was loaded and put it into his waistband and pulled his shirt over it. Walking back out into the road he walked down to the van and pulled it up inside the Americans drive. He lifted the blond in a fireman's carry which caused screaming agony in his shoulder, arms, his dog bitten calf, but he finally got him out of the house and into the back of the van.

Returning to the house he quickly grabbed up more ammunition for the gun as well as his bag and passports. Searching the house, he stopped in a small office, computer room and used the digital camera to take some selfies. He printed them directly from the USB port of the camera to the ink-jet printer and then walked out to the van.

As he started up the van, he heard the blond moving in the back and banging his feet against the locked doors.

"It's my turn to ask the fucking questions now!" Olivier shouted at the man in the back and started the van and drove out of the farmhouse and down the road, heading north again.

Olivier drove for a few hours north following the T1 then turning on to the T2 and pulling off the road near the Kafue river and following a dirt track down to the bank of the river.

Holding the gun ready he opened the back doors of the van. The blond was still tied up, and Olivier grabbed his hair and dragged him out of the van. Using some plastic waxed electrical string he found in the toolbox he tied the mans hand to the bumper of the van, ignoring the man and his pleading.

"I am going to ask you some questions, but unlike your friend Barry I'm not going to torture you. I'm going to believe you because if I think you're lying then I'm just going to kill you."

He pulled the razor knife from his pocket and pressed the tab to slide the triangle of the razor out.

"I'll cut your carotid artery, and you'll bleed out. About twenty-five percent of cardiac output goes to your brain. Most of that blood goes through the carotids, and there are two carotids with let's say about ten percent of cardiac output going through one carotid. So how long it would take you to bleed to death? Any idea?"

Olivier stopped and looked at the man who gulped and looked at him, the fear evident in his eyes. The man shook his head.

"Well, a normal human has a typical cardiac output at rest about five litres per minute. That goes up substantially with activity and stress. Are you under stress?" Olivier asked rhetorically then continued.

"I think it's probably underestimating to double it, but it would give us a conservative estimate. So you'd lose about ten percent of ten litres or one litre of blood per minute through a severed carotid. A person has about seventy millilitres of blood per kilo of body weight, and so for a man your size… say about 100 kg?"

Olivier waited for the man to respond and when the blond nodded slowly he continued.

"That comes out to seven litres of blood. Well before fifty percent blood loss it will be lights out for you, but using fifty percent of seven and one litre per minute, that's three point five minutes for you to bleed out. Or if I cut both about a minute and a half."

Olivier stood up and pointed out across the river.

"I'll dump your body in there and you'll never be found. Now the other option is I believe you, and if I believe you then I'll let you go. You think about it for a minute. I got some work to do with this razor-blade and I don't want any blood on it."

"Listen, I'll tell you whatever you want to know."

Olivier opened up his bag and ignored the man. He took out the selfies he'd taken and two of the fake passports he'd got from Adebayo. Cutting the pictures out carefully he slipped them into the photo pouches of the passport which Adebayo had cut out for them. The problem was he needed an iron or some kind of heat source to close the lamination, so they weren't any use at the moment but it shouldn't be hard to find a hotel somewhere or somewhere to buy a travel iron.

He put the passports away and counted out what was left of his money, it wasn't much, but he did have the bank book. The problem of course is he didn't know who was looking for him or how the Americans had found him.

Time to find out.

Olivier sat down cross-legged on the ground across from Blondie and nodded.

"OK, now it is time for some answers. First I want to know who you work for and why you believe I have a memory stick."

"I work for the CIA, and we were told to pick you up because you might know where the memory stick was." The man leaned forward, eager to please. "We were told to question you and find out which of the two French spies had the memory stick and where it was hidden on the boat."

Olivier sat thoughtfully looking at the man. *Two French spies, interesting, obviously Luc but who is the other?*

"What is on this memory stick?"

"We don't know, they didn't tell us any of that." When Olivier didn't respond, the man repeated himself. "Really, they didn't tell us, that is need to know shit."

"How did you find me?"

"We knew you crossed the border in South Africa, and we were told to wait at the train station, there are other teams covering the other train stations."

"All the train stations?"

"No only the ones closest to the Zimbabwe border, there aren't enough people to cover them all."

"How many agents in the country?"

"Twelve."

Olivier walked to the man who flinched away. Olivier took the gun out before cutting the strings holding the American to the bumper.

"I believe you, now disappear before I decide to change my mind."

Olivier watched the man walking down the road towards the T2 motorway then got into the van and drove past the American. Back on the motorway he sped up and raced northward.

Need to get to the Tanzanian border before they closed it.

CHAPTER FOURTEEN

...

"Barry!" scarface shouted over his shoulder and he looked out the window of the farm house. "We got national police. One car, two locals, one in uniform."

"I'm ready," Barry said checking the clip in his pistol and shoving it into his belt.

"Don't do anything, just bluff it out. The local PD don't know shit, just smile and act like a tourist." Scarface flicked the collar of Barry's Hawaiian shirt as he walked past. He looked out of the window beside the front door and then opened the door and stepped on to the porch."

"Hello officers, how can I help you?"

The uniformed man stepped aside and allowed his superior to walk past him and up the stairs of the porch.

"Hello, we are asking some questions in the area about a missing vehicle."

"Afraid we don't know anything about that," said scarface.

"Can we talk inside?" the policeman said. He held up his badge for scarface to look at. Scarface took the badge and looked at it closely. He was trying to stall for time, while Barry shutdown the computer and stashed any weapons.

"Certainly." Scarface stepped aside and held the door open, but the cop in civilian clothes simply waited for him to go first, then both policemen stepped into the house.

"This is my friend Barry." Scarface said. "We're just renting this house for a month, and we haven't seen any cars round. Other than our rental van of course."

"May I please see your passports and visa?" the cop stood beside Scarface and held his hand out. His partner in uniform walked to the left of the room and turned round to face the men. Barry looked at him nervously since the uniform was standing sideways to them all.

"Sure, sure. No problem. Barry, can you get our passports out of the desk?" Scarface smiled at the cop.

Suddenly the cop in the civilian clothes whipped up a 9mm and pointed it at Scarface's head. Before Barry could react the second policeman had his gun out and pointed at Barry.

"Please be kind enough to put your hands on the back of your heads with your fingers laced together."

The two cops waited until the men had done so, all the while Scarface was protesting his innocence. The uniform cop moved forward and did a quick body search, pulling out Barry's gun and a knife from Scarface's boot.

"Please be seated on the sofa."

Scarface shrugged his shoulders and sat down. Barry sat beside him on the sofa. While the cop in the civilian clothes held them at gunpoint, the other cop searched the house quickly and thoroughly.

"Nothing, nobody else here."

The civilian cop pulled over a kitchen chair and sat down in front of Barry. From his pocket he removed a silencer and attached it to the end of his pistol. He grinned at Barry and then pointed the gun at his head.

"Yesterday at this farm were four men, both of you and two other men. One of these men was a Frenchman, the other, your colleague. Where are these men now?"

"I don't know what you are talk..."

The gun fired, sounding like the dull thud of someone hitting a mattress with a baseball bat. Blood splattered from Barry's head and the entire wall of the farm house was doused in blood. Scarface put his hand to his left cheek, bits of brain and blood were stuck on his face. The civilian cop moved his chair over and sat in front of Scarface.

"Yesterday at this farm were four men, both of you and two other men. One of these men was a Frenchman, the other, your colleague. Where are these men now?"

"The Frenchman escaped, and," he pointed at Barry's body. "We went searching for him. He came back and kidnapped the other guy and took his money and passports. He also took some guns, so he is armed."

The gun went off again and Scarface's blood joined Barry's on the wall, dull red streaks running down the bright flower wall paper. The civilian cop turned and spoke in French.

"Load up the computer and all the documents you can find into the back of the car, then call it in. Resisting arrest, and put the gun back in his hand."

The uniform cop nodded and while he was loading up the computer equipment the civilian cop made a call on his mobile phone to Paris.

"Oui, c'est fini. He didn't need us. He escaped himself."

Gregor Whitley walked into a small cafe in Rome directly across from the Colosseum. He waited at a small table and ordered an espresso while he waited. It wasn't long before two men appeared one walking with a cane and another man who was helping him down the road. Gregor stood and invited the man to sit.

"Bonjourno Gregor, Come stai?" the man asked quietly in Italian.

"Je bein, Carlos," Gregor replied in French and sat down after the older man had made himself comfortable. "It is good to see you my friend."

"Yes, it is good this business has brought us together before I pass on."

"You'll outlive us all." Gregor laughed and put his hand over the older mans hand. "At least it is my wish."

The two old friends sat and chatted about past times and old friends before Gregor moved the meeting on to its purpose.

"I have a favour to ask my friend. It is a favour from the Cosa Nostra to Les Retraités, we would like you to rescind a death warrant for a member of the Legion."

"Enrico Minetti or his younger brother, Stephano?" the old man asked astutely. "It must be the younger brother, because neither the father nor the elder son would ever be forgiven."

"We ask this favour for Stephano Minetti, now known as Olivier Pinson." Gregor said very formally. "He will be of use to Les Retraités. We ask this favour in return for our favour granted in Córdoba."

The old man nodded and the two men began to enjoy their coffee and speak of the old days when they were both in the Legion. Gregor believing they had completed their meeting stood to leave, but the old man put his hand on Gregor's arm.

"Friend, we agree to this favour for Les Retraités, and Stephano Minetti can live without fear of his former brothers in the Cosa Nostra, but he must do a penance to the family which was wronged by his father and brother. There will be no forgiveness without penance. You must tell Stephano, and he must return to Napoli in person."

"I understand friend. I will arrange it.

Gregor walked out of the cafe and towards the metro. He checked his watch; his train would be leaving in two hours. He didn't want to miss it, because he hated flying and would prefer the time to think on the train.

Behind him in the café, the old man called over his assistant. He gripped the younger man's hand with great strength.

"Stephano and Enrico Minetti are still a threat; I want them killed, but find a contractor, someone not associated with us. Les Retraités must never know we didn't grant their favour."

Lieutenant-colonel Robert Birr, Lieutenant commander of the 13e Régiment de Dragons Parachutistes, marched into the offices of the DGSE just as he marched everywhere. He'd been commanded to appear in front of the Director of the DGSE by his commander, who also ordered him to appear in civilian clothes. But even when dressed in trousers and a casual blazer Lieutenant-colonel Birr was unmistakably military. His men often joked that Lieutenant-colonel Birr had been born with a flagpole up his ass and the French drapeau fully unfurled.

The Lieutenant-colonel stepped into the directors office and marched to the desk and stood at parade rest.

"Ah, Lieutenant-colonel Birr, I'm glad you could make it." The director stood up from behind his desk and moved round to shake the mans hand. There was a very awkward moment when the director thought the Lieutenant-colonel would salute not shake his hand, but the Lieutenant-colonel managed to shove his hand out awkwardly. The director managed to extract his hand from the Lieutenant-colonel's vice grip with only a slightly painful grimace.

"Lieutenant-colonel Birr, please be seated, do you mind if I call you, Robert?"

The Lieutenant-colonel nodded and the director continued.

"I've asked you here today because I have something I would like you to do for me. I need to have some men on the ground to reconnoitre a possible extremist threat. Of course this is highly sensitive."

"I believe sir you should direct your request to my commander. I would be happy to pass on your orders."

The director sighed.

"Yes, well. I don't really want to go to the bother of issuing an official request and an official order. I was hoping you and I could work out the request without all the paperwork."

The Lieutenant-colonel sat down slowly in the leather chair beside the director's desk. He put his hand over his mouth and pulled it down over his chin and throat. Suddenly the Lieutenant-colonel felt like he was trapped in a mine-field. His mouth dried, and he began to lick his lips.

"Would it be possible to have some water sir?" the Lieutenant-colonel asked pointing, at the jug of water and the glasses on the director's desk.

"Of course, forgive me for being such a poor host, Robert."

The Lieutenant-colonel milked the glass of water for a long time, he needed to think.

This is a political arena, a jungle with which

I'm not familiar. An unofficial and unauthorised request if delivered discreetly would guarantee my advancement, but if blundered could mean dismissal or even prison in the worst case. Now I understood why the commander hadn't come himself. I will be the scapegoat if things went wrong, and the commander would be free to deny all knowledge. Of course the director wouldn't put anything in writing. He felt his eyes watering. *Strange the reactions to stress. Well, Robert, are you in the game or not?*

"Yes, sir. What would you like us to do?" said Lieutenant-colonel Birr, committing himself and putting the glass of water back down on the table.

"I need to have some men inserted into Somalia and I need to have an ex-Legionnaire terminated."

CHAPTER FIFTEEN

...

Olivier dumped the van just outside of the city of Lusaka and thumbed a ride into the city with some workers in a small flatbed Toyota lorry. It was an enjoyable ride with two of the men able to speak French they laughed and joked the entire trip, and because he said he was heading for Tanzania they told him to stay on-board, they were driving up to Kapiri-Mposhi and it would be easier to get the train from there. He slept on the ground under the lorry with them and in the early afternoon they dropped him off near the TAZARA station to buy tickets.

Olivier stood and waved at the men, then walked into the offices and waited in the queue. Finally, after thirty minutes or so he was in front of the teller and asked for a ticket to Dar es Salaam only to be told that the trains were fully booked for the next two weeks. He attempted to bribe her, but the woman was adamant. There wasn't anyway to get a ticket; everything was booked even the 3rd class bunks.

With a sigh Olivier asked the woman if there was a Barclays bank nearby, she scribbled some instructions on a bit of paper and Olivier walked away from the teller and looked round the station. It would be difficult to board the train without a ticket. He remembered the taxi driver who'd told him he'd have to steal a ticket. He stood observing the people waiting to board the train. It would be difficult to steal a ticket unless you killed or incapacitated the ticket holder so badly they couldn't speak for days. It would take hours waiting for the train.

So while standing at the teller station he'd seen the bank book when looking for his passport and remembered the money. He didn't have to steal a ticket, he had more than enough money to scalp a ticket from someone.

There were a number of Americans and

Europeans as well as locals waiting for the train so he decided that he would get both local currently and Euro. Walking outside it was easy to find a taxi driver who would take him to the Bank and wait outside for him to return.

The trip to the bank and back although hassle free was time consuming and the train had already pulled into the station. Boarding would begin soon.

He stood for a moment and looked round the station. There were three young men obviously college students, who were collecting up their backpacks and chatting as they waited in the long line which was forming to board. Olivier decided to approach them first.

"Bonjour." Olivier said trying to look as winsome as possible.

"Salut comment ça va," replied the taller one in French.

"You're French?" Olivier asked, glad to be able to use French and not struggle with English for a change.

"No, We're from Belgium actually."

"I wonder if I can impose on you? I have a very important meeting in Dar es Salaam, in three days' time, but my secretary in Paris couldn't book the ticket online. So I don't have a ticket and I really need to get on this express train."

The men looked at him nervously, they were obviously wary of being tricked or conned.

"I wondered if I could buy your tickets off of you. I will pay you one thousand Euro per ticket."

The men glanced at each other and the tall one spoke.

"Do you have the money?"

Having already anticipated this question Olivier opened the top of his backpack and allowed them to look at the neatly wrapped bills inside.

"I can give you the money here, but I don't think you would want to let everyone know that you have that much money on you. If you agree we can go there," Olivier pointed at a small alcove in the corner of the station. "It is still in public, so you nor I don't have to worry about either of us not keeping our end of the bargain, and discreet enough so nobody can see we have money."

The men whispered briefly to each other and they nodded and Olivier followed them to the alcove. They handed him a ticket, which he inspected and then bought them all so he would have a carriage to himself.

Olivier got back in line and waved at the three youngsters when they waved at him and left the station. They were almost dancing as they walked out of the station. Olivier grinned, he'd probably given them more money than they'd had in months. Poor travelling students with three grand in their pocket.

The room was a first class berth with four bunks and a table. The toilet was basic with only a bucket of water to flush. The taps in the washroom provided a small drip to wash his hands.

Because he was on the express train, he would be in Dar es Salaam in 48-56 hours. He didn't have any food, so he flagged down the carriage attendant and had him lock his cabin while he moved down to the dining car.

Olivier asked what the options were for dinner.

"Chicken and rice."

"Anything else?"

"All we have is chicken and rice."

"Bon, chicken and rice please."

Olivier found a seat and ate the chicken and rice and bought a dozen beers from the bar. There was no running water on the train and he hadn't purchased any food or water before travelling.

He went back to his cabin and opened the small toilet which stunk of urine and using the dripping tap on the sink and an old shirt washed as the wildlife and countryside passed in the window. It was an odd contrast the lovely scenery at dusk and the stink of urine.

He pulled the bandages off his wounds and examined them. Opening the beer, he drank it back completely and then peeled away all the bandages. Using the dripping water and a roll of clean gauze which he'd purchased at a pharmacy on the way to the station.

Pity I didn't buy some food, he thought shaking his head.

He took out a small bottle of disinfectant wash and with a new piece of gauss cleaned and irrigated all the wounds on his chest and leg. Then bandaged each one up with clean bandages. Finally, feeling relatively clean and refreshed he drank another warm beer with a couple of aspirins and lay down on a bunk to get some sleep.

Olivier discovered sleeping on the Tazara train is an interesting experience. Even when at standstill he could feel the carriages crashing together and was constantly being shoved round in his seat/bunk. He assumed this happened whenever carriages were added or removed at points along the journey, but he never did find out why. Olivier's first nights sleep was broken either by the train stopping, starting, creaking and jarring or a guard knocking on the door to tell him to secure the window.

But even broken sleep helped him to wake up feeling refreshed but hungry. As he waved down the attendant to lock his cabin, he remembered an American film he'd once seen in the Legion, one of the characters had said.

"I'm so hungry, my stomach thinks my throats been cut."

Olivier thought he could sympathise. He hurried down to the food carriage to see what was on offer for breakfast.

"Omelette."

"Anything else?" Olivier said.

"All we have is omelette."

"Bon, I'll have omelette."

Olivier rolled his eyes and stuffed the dry omelette down his throat, and because he was so hungry ordered another.

Olivier spent the rest of the day in his cabin sipping beer and that evening eating chicken and rice from the dining car.

The next morning the train stopped for almost two hours outside of a village, and everyone within a hundred miles seemed to descend on the train selling anything from telephone SIM cards to bananas. But the fruit sellers were a god send to Olivier who purchased a huge sack of fruit. A diet of omelette, chicken and rice didn't have the variety he craved.

The landscape began to change as the train neared Tanzania. The flat golden ground of Zambia gave way to lush green hills and in the afternoon of day two the train crossed the border. The train stopped, and border guards moved through the train checking visas and passports.

Olivier had both a visa, and passport thanks to Adebayo, but it would have been easy enough to purchase a visa. A number of passengers in the dining car did.

Looking out the window of the dining car, Olivier observed three men who were clustered together a few carriages down from where he was sitting. The men split up, one going to the head of the train, the other entering the middle and the other walking back down the length of the train. As the man passed the dining car, Olivier could see the lump of a handgun under the mans shirt tucked into the small of his back.

"Merde," Olivier swore softly, his cabin was locked and he didn't have any weapons on him. The gun was still in his backpack. He quietly slipped the knife and fork from his plate and put them into his trouser pockets. He stood and began to make his way through the crowded carriage, past the border guards towards his cabin.

He almost made it back to his cabin. He'd just entered his carriage when one of the men walked through the door at the other end of the carriage. The man was shorter than Olivier but muscular with a V-shaped torso, and close cropped hair. Olivier tried to bluff his way and just continue walking.

"Bonjour, Monsieur Pinson." The man said in French and held up one hand, the other behind his back.

Olivier looked at the man and then

glanced behind him as a second man appeared at the back of the carriage. The man pulled a knife, which Olivier immediately identified as the 13cm Poignard-Commando. A solid steel black matte knife issued to combat troops. This man was also short, but more oriental looking than the first man. Olivier continued his bluff, but put his hand into his pockets putting the fork into his left hand and the butter knife into the right.

"Sorry I don't speak French," Olivier replied in Italian walking close to the French speaker. He could sense the man behind him approaching.

"Don't move, you're coming with us," the first man said.

Olivier's hands flashed out of his pockets and he slammed his forearms into the man's hands knocking them wide and stepping forward he hammered his forehead directly into the man's nose. Blood spurted instantly and Olivier brought his knee up into the man's groin for good measure. He spun quickly, the second man was bringing his knife in low in a sweeping arc aiming for the belly.

Olivier stepped back slightly to avoid the

blow and when the blade had past, stepped in and stuck the fork into the man's arm. He continued to shove the fork and the man's arm to his right, while he rotated keeping his back to the wall. The other man moved away from Olivier and put his back to the window of the carriage.

Olivier's hands flashed out towards the man, but his blows were met and returned rapid-fire. Both men were well trained in close quarter fighting. Elbows, knees, fists flashed back and forth as each fought for advantage. Olivier struggled to keep the poignard away. The sharp combat knife gave his attacker the advantage.

Olivier deflected the poignard away from his face using the fork. Olivier's other hand flicked the butter knife towards the man's eye. He batted the butter knife away, but Olivier brought the fork down on to the top of his wrist. The fork sunk deep striking the bones of the wrist. Olivier's hand was near the man's head and Olivier dropped the butter knife and grabbed the man's hair, yanking his head towards him and cracking his forehead into the man's nose.

Holding on to his hair and the hand holding the knife he swept the man's head into the wall behind him. Olivier kicked out with his foot and the same time, trying to sweep his legs out from under him.

As the man began falling, Olivier saw the French speaker getting off the floor and aiming a silenced pistol. Olivier pulled the knife-man in front of him as the Frenchman fired. The thud of the gun was loud in the small carriage corridor. Olivier shoved the knife-man away and at the Frenchman. The Frenchman was knocked backward when the weight of his comrade hit him. Olivier flung himself over the body of the knife-man and brought his elbow down directly into the forehead of the Frenchman. The man blinked hard, dazed.

Olivier grabbed the hand the gun was in forcing the gun barrel away from him and striking the man's throat repeatedly with his fist.

Olivier stood looking at the two men. One was dead from the gunshot wound and the other man dying from asphyxiation. He kicked open the door to his cabin and dragged the bodies into the room. He stepped outside and looked round. Picking up the gun and the knife, he threw them into the cabin. It seemed amazing but it was only two or three minutes since the first man had spoken.

Gotta hide them, he thought, *but where?*

Olivier took some bottled water and splashed it quickly over the blood stains and mopped it up with a shirt. He closed the door and did his best to fix the lock. After he had secured the door to the cabin, he opened the toilet and shoved the bodies of the men into it.

The train jerked and began to move. Olivier closed the door of the toilet and sat down on the bunk. He picked up one of his warm beers and downed it completely.

How the hell am I going to get rid of these two? And where is the other one? Still on the train?

After he'd drank his beer and calmed a little Olivier opened the toilet and searched the men, taking out their passports and documents. He opened them, then sank slowly down on his bunk the passport and papers falling out of his hands.

Merde! 13eme Regiment de Dragons Parachutistes! What were they doing trying to kidnap me? Why attack me? Everyone is against me. They all believe I'm the second spy on the yacht.

CHAPTER SIXTEEN

...

Marie was unchained from the pole in the middle of the warehouse and two men stood guard with guns while a third lead her to the house. At the door the maid opened the door, and Marie was directed to sit in the chair at the table.

After a few moments Emile walked into the room and told the woman to get some food and coffee and ordered the men to leave. All left except one swarthy looking bearded man with long hair.

"My dear Marie, I hope you have rested from your little adventure?"

"Yes, I am wonderfully well rested." Marie replied equally sarcastically. "What do you want?"

"You know what I want, I want the memory stick but unfortunately your boss didn't know the location of it. I believe you have it, or at least know where it is."

Marie smiled at him and then lifted her hands up to display the handcuffs. Emile waved and the bearded man moved over quickly and removed the handcuffs.

"I suppose I might as well tell you," Marie said as the man was taking off the handcuffs, "After all you seem to already know."

"Exactly," he said.

"It is still on the boat."

Emile just laughed and the woman appeared with the tray of sandwiches and coffee. Emile poured himself a strong coffee and gestured for Marie to eat.

"Actually I know it isn't on the boat, because you see the CIA have had the boat lifted from the ocean floor by the US Navy, and the entire yacht has been gone through with a fine tooth comb. The divers have searched the entire area; it isn't on the boat."

"I don't have it." Marie said, her mind twirling at this information about the CIA and wondering if it was true.

"Yes, I know that as well. After your escape I had your shed, your belongings and everything in or round this camp searched. I even had the shed you and your boss were held in taken down board by board and searched. I had the sand sifted through inside and round the shed just for good measure."

Marie took as sandwich and chewed while she thought. Emile continued.

"I know you were given the memory stick, this information was volunteered by your boss before he died. So I know you had it when you arrived here, and since your escape it cannot be found. Therefore, I can only conclude you have hidden it somewhere between here and where you were found."

"I don't have it." she said. Emile ignored her and continued to talk.

"I've dispatched men to track where you've been and to look for the memory stick. I've also offered money to all the locals for its return. More money than they will see in ten years. And finally I'm talking to you."

"You can torture me, but I still cannot tell you what you want to know, because I don't know where it is."

"I'm not going to torture you, I'm going to

recruit you. You see the French government has ordered me to kill you and your husband."

He smiled at the look on Marie's face.

"Yes, it appears your husband escaped from the hospital, has broken laws in a number of countries, illegally crossed a few of borders and is on his way here. But given the number of people looking for him, I seriously doubt he will succeed without help."

Emile stopped and lit a cigarette while this information was proceeded by her.

"Help only I can give him. You see, I can send men to meet him, escort him here to you. I can have you living in America under assumed names by the end of the week."

"Assuming I know where this memory stick is, why would the Americans be interested?"

"I don't know, and I don't care. But they will pay for the memory stick, and if it means arranging for some agents to be taken to the USA, then they'll do it."

Marie sat and picked up another sandwich and chewed it.

It doesn't surprise me the French government wouldn't pay, but what is on this memory stick they would be willing to kill their own agent in order to ensure it is lost? Surely they would rather rescue me? Poor Olivier doesn't know I got him into this mess. I couldn't tell him I was an agent, but I couldn't. I could have quit, but you can't really quit once you're in you're in.

"I will let you think about it. Jameel will show you to a room, and you can shower and dress. I've asked the maid to provide you with some local clothing. I want you to think about your husband, he is being hunted like a dog and if we act now we can save him."

Jameel lead her to a room down a small hallway and gestured for her to enter. Inside on the bed was a long black berka and some underwear which looked as if they would fit her. The door behind her closed as another door opened and the maid appeared. A puff of steam emerged from the door along with the woman and behind her Marie could see a toilet.

"There is a bath." The woman said in broken English and pointed at the bed. "I have you the clothes."

"Merci, thank you."

Marie walked into the toilet and touched

the water in the bathtub. It was scalding hot and ready. She smiled, and the woman closed the door behind her. Marie stripped off the filthy clothes with days of sand and sweat on them and climbed into the bath. She sighed as the hot water covered her body and she lay back enjoying the heat.

If what he says is true, I should do the deal, she thought, but remembered the voice of her instructor.

One of the first principles of captivity is to never, ever believe anything your captor says unless you see it with your own eyes, and even then you should be sceptical.

All agents went through a training in evasion and capture. They were dumped in the middle of nowhere with only a map and rendezvous points to hit. They spent a week trying to evade the French army, who were also on exercise and instructed to capture them. In the second week, regardless if they'd evaded capture or not they were taken to a POW simulation. They were tricked, starved, given mock executions, anything could be done to prepare them for capture short of actual torture.

Marie leaned forward and picked up a sponge and cleaned herself as best she could. She was really worried about Olivier. He'd never known what her real role in the DGSE really was. He had assumed she was in some kind of management or administration position. She knew her captors would mix truth with lies in order to get what they wanted. She felt Olivier escaping prison and coming north to look for her was true. That was the type of man he was. Hell, high water, Somalian pirates, or the devil himself wouldn't keep Olivier from coming to rescue her.

The only leverage I have is the memory stick. Nobody gives a monkeys ass about me or Olivier, anymore than they cared about Luc. I stay alive as long as only I know where the memory stick is. It will be hard for them to find, but not impossible. I will tell him I'll give him the memory stick when Olivier is here, not before. It will buy me time and hopefully keep Olivier safe. If he is bluffing about Olivier, then I'll know.

Marie emerged from the bath clean and scrubbed. There was no towel in the toilet. She sighed.

Looks like I'll have to 'air dry'

She opened the door a crack and looked round. The woman had left, and the clothes were still on the bed. Marie stepped out into the room. The air was much cooler here and goosebumps began to rise on her skin. The room was small, with only a dressing table and a small chest of drawers. She quickly walked over to the chest of drawers and opened each hoping for a towel, but all the drawers were empty.

I'll put them on wet.

Marie walked back towards the bed when the door to the corridor opened and the man Jameel entered. He grinned as he looked at her naked. She instinctively moved her hands down to cover herself.

"Get out!" she ordered, but the man ignored her and laughed. He walked towards her and Marie backpedaled behind the bed trying to put some distance between them. The man lunged forward and grabbed her shoulder. He jerked her back round and slapped her across the face brutally. The pain exploded across her cheek and she felt some blood inside of her mouth.

Marie screamed as the man shoved her backwards and she fell on to the bed. Marie pulled her feet back and kicked as hard as she could into the man's chest.

"Ohffffff" the breath expelled from the

mans chest and he dropped down to one knee. Marie clipped him in the jaw with the heel of her foot. She rolled towards the side off the bed and off, trying to get to her feet quickly. As she stood up, the sound of a gunshot rocked the room. She saw a cloud of blood as the man's head exploded in a mist of red.

Standing at the door and holding a pistol was Emile.

"I'm glad to see you are unharmed." He gestured behind him and the woman entered. "Put her in my room and get her some new clothes, those have blood on them."

Emile pushed the maid into the room. He paused to look at Marie and grinned. She stood naked hands on her hips glaring at him. He spun and walked back to his office closing the door behind him. He called his lieutenant and told him to have the body removed. On the cameras he watched the guest room and as they lead Marie out to another room he flicked the view over to his own room.

Nice choice brother, he thought as he watched

the naked woman. She certainly has backbone, perhaps I will actually ask the CIA to save her. No, to much hassle.

Emile laughed and then gulped down some more coffee. The two women entered the room but didn't speak. He could hear them moving round the room, so he knew the microphones were working. He watched her get dressed and then after the other woman left Marie looked through the room looking for weapons or and escape. But there was nothing in the room of use to her, he'd already checked it.

In the other room two men were taking out Jameel's body and the woman was washing out the blood. *It is a pity he had to die, but still it served a purpose. She knows she is dependent on me, and that here I rule over life or death.*

He read through his emails, but his mind was thinking about the womans escape. The memory stick must have been on her when she came, but stupidly he'd not had them searched. An oversight which he was paying for heavily now. He had all the worlds intelligence agencies against him, but no leverage without the memory stick.

"Merde!"

Emile picked up the coffee pot and threw it against the wall.

I have to find that fucking memory stick, and if this bitch has to die then so be it!

CHAPTER SEVENTEEN

...

The train arrived in Dar es Salaam twenty-four hours after Olivier had stuffed the bodies into the toilet. He'd not seen anything of the third man. He wondered if he could leave the train the moment it stopped or wait until it was empty. However, the longer he waited the quicker they would find the bodies after he got off the train. He'd decided to have his things packed and ready to go. Olivier had repaired the lock on the door of the cabin and spent the night using the commando knife to carve out a small wedge from some wood he'd broken off the bunk. He tied a string to the small end of the wedge. As soon as the train stopped he put his bag outside of the door and then using the string he pulled the wedge against the door.

Hopefully, this would delay the opening of the door for a few more minutes. Pushing against the door would only wedge it tighter. He cut the string and put the knife into his bag. Throwing the bag over his shoulder, he moved quickly to the door of the train and shoved and shouldered his way through the crowd of people waiting to disembark.

He walked out of the train station and walked over to the taxi rank. There was a long queue of cabs waiting in the queue. Olivier walked to the back of the queue to the last driver. He leaned into the window with a one hundred euro note in his hand.

"I don't want to wait in this queue. I know it is against the rules, but I'll make it worth your while."

The driver looked at the money, then took a hard long look at him. Olivier had to blink his eyes; the man stank of garlic.

"Certainly, jump in. I'll call my dispatcher and let him know I've got a fare."

Olivier handed the man the note and jumped in the back. The taxi pulled away from the taxi rank and some of the drivers raised a hand in protest, but the driver drove on, driving with one hand and talking on the phone in Arabic with the other. Olivier leaned forward to talk to him after he had hung up the phone.

"I need to charter a boat and I need to get some equipment. I can make it worth your while."

"Sure, no problem. I know someone who charters boats, I'll call him."

Olivier sat back in the taxi and relaxed a little. The driver was calling on the phone, speaking in rapid-fire Arabic, and dodging seemly crazed drivers on narrow twisting streets. The driver hung up his phone and looked back at Olivier talking. The man didn't bother to look round at the road and Olivier began to feel his ass squirm on the seat.

"My friend has a boat, not problem. Any size you want. Good price for you my friend."

"Great. Ahh, can you watch the road?"

The man laughed and turned back to look at the road. They drove for about ten minutes before arriving into a run down part of the sea port. To his left Olivier saw the huge ocean going container ships that were docked in the port. Huge cranks were working over the ships, and long flatbed lorries waited to receive their loads.

The driver pulled away from the port and turned on a small road leading to what looked like a run down warehouses.

"My friend, he is here. The boats are in the port, but you have to see him in the office. I will wait for you."

"Merci."

"With the meter running," the man completed his sentence and gave a chuckle. Olivier laughed.

"OK, I understand. What is your friends name?"

"Ask for Ahmed."

The driver pulled up to the warehouse and pointed at a small metal door inside of the larger hanger door. The driver got out of the car and pulled a cigarette from his pocket and lit it.

"Hurry, the meter is running."

Olivier chuckled and put his hand on the strap of his bag but then left it on the seat. He walked over to the metal door and slid the bolt back. The door opened and Olivier stepped in, the warehouse was pitch-black and he tried to adjust his eyes to the dark interior.

The back of his head erupted in pain as something came down on it. Olivier saw stars, but his training took over and he lunged forward tucking his head into his left shoulder and rolling over his right shoulder and on to his back, then jumping up to his feet.

Around him in the blurry darkness he could just see five or more men rushing at him. He reached round and yanked the silenced gun he took off the man yesterday. He pointed the gun at the nearest man not even bothering to aim.

Thud. The sound of the silenced gun wasn't a deterrent to the men. Although they saw the flash of light, they didn't seem to notice their comrade fold up and fall to his knees. Olivier ran at the man he'd just shot and dodged round him through the only gap. He moved the gun round smoothly aiming as he ran and shot another one of the men in the forehead.

His eyes were now accustomed to the darkness, and he could see ahead of him bales of something, possibly straw, or marijuana he couldn't know. Suddenly a shot burst out behind him and he dived to his left between some bales. He looked carefully over the bale and aimed at one of the shifting shapes in the darkness.

The shape fell to the ground and a two more shots rang out throwing up puffs of dust in the bale were Olivier was hiding. He quickly began to crawl away as a machine gun opened up on the bale where he'd just been. The flashing light from the muzzle gave Olivier a good target, and he fired twice. Someone screamed. Olivier stood stooped over and ran towards the back of the warehouse. Shifting back and forth between the bales.

How many are there?

He stopped for a moment and put his back to a pile of bales four high. He could hear three maybe as many as four voices. They were more cautious now, and they were moving systematically through the bales. Olivier tucked the gun back into his waistband and climbed up the bales. He lay there on his stomach and pulled the gun out. Peering down over the side of the bales, he could see shapes moving through the gridded corridors between the bales. Two of the shapes were approaching his position together and another was farther away to his right. He took the pistol in both hands and waited until he could see the pair of men approaching his hiding place.

Thud, thud.

Two shots and two men down.

The machine gun opened fire on his position after the flashes from his gun had given away his location. He rolled off the bales and landed awkwardly on his foot and dropping the gun in the darkness. The machine gunner was running towards his position and firing as he came. Olivier lay on the ground sweeping his hand back and forth trying to get a hold of the gun. The machine gun stopped, and Olivier touched the gun barrel just as the man walked round the corner. The machine gun was pointed up towards the top of the bales, and the man was looking up. The scraping sound of the gun as Olivier dragged it towards him attracted the man's attention.

Olivier swung his foot out and kicked the man in the knee as he spun. Holding the pistol, he took a quick shot. The bullet hit the man in the hip and spun him round. One last shot into his head and Olivier grabbed the machine gun and crept back towards the door at the front of the warehouse.

He stepped out of the door and looked round. The taxi was driving off and he could see it speeding off down the road. He walked round the warehouse but there were no vehicles round. Olivier threw the machine gun into a ditch and then checked the pistol. One round left.

"You bastard."

Olivier looked at the speeding taxi as it drove away with his money and passports. The road the taxi driver was on was a single tracked road with a ditch on each side. The driver wouldn't be able to turn until he got to the main port road they had come up. Olivier started running across the parking lot and leaped the ditch. He ran across the open ground.

The taxi would have drive down the road which curved right and across the field which Olivier was running. He sprinted as fast as he could, the taxi wasn't driving fast and Olivier doubted the driver had seen him or knew he was being chased down.

Pain flared up from his ankle, the fall from the bales hadn't been without injury. The run was giving him excruciating pain as he ran across the rocky ground. Over to his left he could see the taxi approaching the start of the curve. The driver would be able to see him soon moving across the field. Olivier needed to get to the road before the man sped up and escaped.

Olivier gritted his teeth and taking great gulping breaths of the blazing hot air tried to pick up even more speed. His lungs burned and his right ankle screamed with pain. He could feel the wounds in his chest opening and tears streamed from his eyes, the wet salty tears tailing back down his cheek.

Olivier was nearing the road now. The ditch was just ahead of him. The taxi was speeding up, the dust and rocks spitting out of the back of the car. Olivier leaped the ditch and landed on his bad ankle. He fell forward and rolled onto his shoulder. He heard the car coming, and stood as quickly as he could yanking the gun out. Pointing it at the car, he fired. The bullet shattered the windscreen and the car swerved to the side of the road and hit the ditch. A huge spray of dirt and rocks flew up into the air. The taxi driver opened the door and climbed out of the car.

"Don't move!" Olivier shouted pointing the empty gun at his head. "Get on the fucking ground if you want to live."

The driver stopped and put his hands on his head, facing away from Olivier, the driver slowly dropped to his knees and put his hands behind his head. Olivier walked up behind him and using his foot shoved the man down on to the ground.

"Don't kill me!" the man pleaded.

"Shut up."

Olivier walked to the car and opened the back door while holding the empty gun towards the man, who was watching him from the ground. Olivier took his bag and put it over his shoulder. Then hobbled back down towards the man. His ankle throbbed and ached so badly he was almost unable to walk.

"Why?"

"Don't kill me," the man whispered tears rolled down his cheek.

"Why did they try to kill me? Who are you? Who are they? Were you specifically looking for me?"

"Your picture has been given to all the taxi drivers in the city. Someone would have brought you here. Please don't kill me. I just needed the money."

"Who were they? Why did they want me?"

"I don't know, they are Somalian."

Olivier moved the silenced barrel of the gun down and tapped the man on the forehead.

"I'm going to walk down this road towards the port. You can get up off the ground when you cannot see me anymore. If you can get your car out of the ditch, then drive away. Otherwise, you can walk in the opposite direction. But don't let me see you again. If I see you again then you die. If someone tells me you have told anyone about me, then I'll kill you. In fact, why shouldn't I kill you now?"

"No please! I promise, I will forget your face, or I've ever seen you. I will never tell anyone about you."

Olivier walked away from the car and across the broken ground towards the main port road. He wanted to get away from the warehouse and the taxi driver as quickly as possible. As he walked, he wiped down the pistol and then threw the pistol to the ground. He stopped for a moment and looked back towards the driver. The man was still on the ground. He turned and continued to trudge down the road. His ankle throbbed like hell and he could feel his chest bleeding.

He arrived at a crossroads to the port road and walking along it looked at the rise of the tall cranes and ships. Along the road there was a lot more traffic. Lorries, goods vehicles, and motorcycles zipped along past him. Further up the road he could see a cluster of small buildings and a cafe sign.

Well, get a coffee and maybe I can find a phone to call Cyrille.

The cafe was typical of its type worldwide. A long high bar ran along one wall and behind it worked the fry cook and the waiter. There were four tables on the other side of the bar, all with plastic tablecloths. There were salt and pepper shakers on each table and a sugar dispenser. The tables were all full with men drinking coffee or eating.

Olivier walked to the bar and ordered a coffee he tried to ask about a phone but either they didn't have one, or the waiters English wasn't up to it. Olivier sat at one of the tall stools at the end of the bar and took a sip of his coffee. He said staring into his coffee cup and wondering what he was going to do when he heard someone speaking in French. Looking up he spotted two men near the window who were chatting quietly in French. He gulped down his coffee and walked over to their table.

"Excuse me. I couldn't help but overhear you and wondered if I could ask a favour?"

"You can ask," said one of the men, "but I don't know if we can help."

"I've been robbed by a taxi driver. I just wondered if you could tell me how I can get to the French embassy. Or perhaps somewhere I can make a call to France?" Olivier stood waiting as the two men looked at each other and then the first one spoke.

"You can place a call from my ship to France, but I don't know where the Embassy is here."

Olivier smiled and held his name out to the man, "My name is Olivier."

"This is Gerard, and I'm Alex, we are just leaving for the ship." The man pointed at a large red and black ship which was sitting under a crane while cargo was unloaded from it. "I'm the captain, and Gerard is the first mate."

"I need to charter a boat. You wouldn't

know anyone local who does that?" Olivier asked as they walked towards the man's ship.

"Yes, Pierre lives down here, he rents boats to tourists," Gerard said. "He is an old shipmate of ours, met a local girl and stayed."

"I'm so glad I spoke to you," Olivier said. "I really was afraid I wouldn't be able to find a charter I could trust."

CHAPTER EIGHTEEN

...

Gregor Whitley walked down the Rue du Fouarre and stopped on the corner at a Japanese restaurant. He stood on the corner for a moment looking round to his left, inside a telephone booth, a man in a suit stood talking on the phone, to his right was a telephone company lorry with orange and white cones behind it. Curiously he looked at the man in the suit who stepped into view.

"Bonjour Monsieur Director," Gregor greeted the Director of the DGSE.

"S'il vous plait. Shall we go inside?" The director opened the door of the restaurant and held it open for Gregor. Gregor stopped for a moment and looked at the telephone repair van, and then went inside. The director gave his name, and they were lead to a table in the back by a smiling oriental woman.

"What is the problem Matias?" Gregor said after the woman had handed them the menu and left.

"A man from the 13th draggons was killed on the train to Tansania along with another man. Do you know anything about this?"

"No," Gregor said thoughtfully and then added. "Was it the missing man, Olivier Pinson?"

"No, he hasn't been identified yet. The authorities in Tanzania aren't being very helpful. We don't know the nationality of the man, but the Tanzanians claim he was French and several people overheard him and a third man speaking French before boarding the train."

"Well, this is all very interesting but…" Gregor stopped as the waitress returned and he ordered some sushi and coffee. He waited until the woman left again before speaking. "All very interesting but I fail to see why you've dragged me from my office to tell me about the death of two men I don't know in a country I've never been to."

"Because," the Director said as spittle flew from his lips, "your fucking legionnaire killed them."

"Firstly, this man Olivier Pinson isn't 'my' legionnaire, and secondly, if they've put him in prison for murder it as a matter for the French Embassy in Tanzania, no?"

"Gregor, you're being deliberately obtuse and it is annoying."

Gregor shrugged and the men said silently looking at each other as the oriental woman delivered the food and coffee. Obviously picking up on the cool atmosphere between the two men she made a hasty retreat away from the table.

If they know Olivier has killed two men, it will not be long before they discover Les Retraités is searching for him.

"I think you've had something to do with this, and I personally believe this third man worked for Les Retraités."

Which means my man isn't one of the dead ones and Olivier escaped, he thought.

Gregor drummed his fingers on the table, a gesture he knew would annoy the director. He wondered how much he should tell if anything. If as he suspected the telephone van outside was a surveillance vehicle it would be best to say nothing. He didn't know if they worked for the director or someone else.

"Look here Matias, I'm not going to tell you how to do your job, but it is highly inappropriate for you to drag me out of my office to make unproven accusations about me and my organisation. Les Retraités do not condone or conduct murder in any place or time. We are a retirement advisory organisation and a registered charity. I'm offended."

The director snorted out a derisory laugh and Gregor raised an eye.

"I sent some men to pick up this Olivier Pinson and bring him safely back to France. Somehow these men died and now there are some explanations due. I want this man, Olivier Pinson, returned. If you or anyone in your organisation sees or talks to him, then tell him to report to the nearest French Embassy. Do I make myself clear?"

This was unauthorised. He sent them down there without official paperwork, and now a soldier is dead and people are going to want answers. Poor old Matais is buried deep in shit and is looking for a scapegoat. Either Olivier Pinson or Les Retraités will do.

"I'm sure there will be an enquiry and it will all come out then. Don't worry to much Matias, and if you need another favour from us, perhaps it could be arranged."

"I won't be going to be deeper in your pocket," the Director said between gritted teeth. "I don't need any help from you or your cronies. You just need to get Olivier Pinson to the nearest Embassy."

"Really Matias, is there any need to become impolite? Haven't we only ever helped you? I thought you appreciated the information we released about the previous Director General? After all, you inherited his position."

"Yes, because he wouldn't play ball with Les Retraités. He warned me about you, told me you'd helped get me this position so you could use me like a toy. If only he'd told me before you did me one of your 'favours' then I wouldn't need to skulk round speaking to you."

Gregor drained his coffee and stood. He reached out and put his hand on the director's shoulder.

"I'll have him go to the Embassy if he contacts Les Retraités. Personally I would be willing to forget the favour, but the organisation never forgets favours done for them, or by them. I'll be happy to help you if there is an enquiry, but next time come to my office."

"I'm sure if there is an enquiry into anything I will not need your help." The director brushed Gregor's hand off his shoulder.

"Well, if not us, then perhaps the people in the surveillance van outside disguised as a telephone van will help you."

Gregor laughed silently to himself as he walked away. He knew from the directors face he didn't know, and it probably wasn't the DGSE.

Who is watching the watchers? Gregor stopped outside stood beside the van and lit a cigarette. *I really do love this job.*

Cyrille received a call on his mobile phone from Gregor an hour after Gregor's meeting with the director. Cyrille answered the phone and was listening to Gregor when the director stormed past him towards his office without saying a word.

"If your man calls you tell him to stay

away from any French Embassies, government buildings, etc. The DGSE is after him. I have spoken to the Mafia about him, but my informant tells me although they've agreed to my face to leave Olivier, they plan to kill him."

"Oui." Cyrille says into the phone, walking down the hallway and towards the outside smoking area.

"We cannot provide him with any direct assistance, but we have a man in Tanzania named Husain Morcos who can provide him with a ship and some weapons. Husain has a shop on Kivukoni road."

Cyrille stepped outside and lit a cigarette. The smoking area was empty.

"If he doesn't call me?"

"He is resourceful, he'll either call you, or he'll manage on his own. We cannot contact him directly, my hands have been tied by your director. Also, I believe there is at least one other third party interested in your man. I am under surveillance now as is your director, and possibly you too. Take care."

Gregor hung-up and Cyrille wiped his face with one hand and sighed.

"Merde!"

CHAPTER NINETEEN

...

Olivier called Cyrille from the ships phone and was given the information about the guns and the ships. Cyrille told him that Emile had threatened to kill his wife if he didn't get the money for the memory stick. After that, he would offer the memory stick to the highest bidder.

"What are the coordinates?" Olivier asked and mimed writing to Gerard who handed him a pen and paper. After noting down the coordinates and the Les Retraités contact. He told Cyrille he would call him later tonight from a hotel and hung up the phone.

"Everything alright?" Gerard asked him. "You don't look very well."

Olivier tried to mask his anger and looked

at Gerard and shrugged.

"Bit of bad news about my family, but shouldn't be a problem. I just need an earlier flight than I'd anticipated. Your man with the ships, is he close by?"

"Oh sure, just down the road," Gerard took the pen and paper from Olivier and scribbled the name and address of the man on the paper. "You could walk there, but there are some taxis which stop along the top of the road."

"Well, I don't trust them much, but with my foot hurting it is probably better if I take a taxi. Thanks for all your help."

Gerard looked at him and tapped the navigation table with his finger.

"Those coordinates are in Somalia you know."

Olivier looked at him. They were alone on the bridge.

Who can I trust? Les Retraités probably not. These men, who I have just met? Perhaps.

"Yes, I'm going there to get my wife back."

Gerard nodded and climbed into the navigators chair and gestured for Olivier to sit in the other chair. He sat tugging on his earlobe while Olivier took his seat.

"Alex and I figured you weren't robbed by the taxi driver, or if you'd had some trouble with a taxi driver then he probably came off worse. You look like you have been eaten by a shark and shit out."

Olivier laughed and nodded.

"That is a very accurate description of how I feel."

Alex entered the bridge and put his walkie-talkie on the navigation table. He looked at the two men and leaned on the table and lit a cigarette.

"Having a heart to heart?"

"He was just telling me why he looks like a half eaten pork sandwich." Gerard said.

"I am travelling north into Somalia to get my wife. She was captured by some pirates about a week ago." Olivier tapped on the bit of paper with the coordinates on it. "I'm going to charter a boat and buy some weapons, then I'm going in."

"Alone?" Alex asked. "Isn't that a little more than a bit stupid?"

"Yes. But I don't really have options. The government will not pay a ransom, and they are going to kill her in three days' time."

"That what your friend told you?" Gerard

said. "The one you called?"

"Yes, he works for the government. He got me the location of the camp and told me they're going to kill her. He's given me the name of a man who can sell me some weapons. So I have to go now."

Alex stubbed out his cigarette into the ashtray with one hand and put his right hand into the air.

"I have a question. Why would you tell us?"

Olivier shakes his head. "I don't really know, but I've had some people trying to stop me getting this far and I'm not sure who I can and cannot trust. So, well, I thought you were probably more trustworthy than most of the people who are involved in this."

"D'accord. What can we do to help you?" Alex asked and looked at Gerard who nodded confirmation.

"Well, you said you knew someone who charters boats, someone you trust. If I can get a boat, then I can try to get weapons."

Alex crooked a finger at Olivier and walked to the back of the bridge towards a steel bulkhead door with a large padlock."Well, you said you knew someone who charters boats, someone you trust. Olivier whistled as he went inside. The room was an armoury. There were eight machine guns, a sniper rifle and even a Russian made rocket launcher, and other assorted hardware.

"We decided to defend ourselves when the Somalians were really active with the pirate skiffs," Gerard explained, "Alex and I are joint owners of this ship, it isn't a freight franchise, it is ours. We were thinking of selling it all because the piracy has almost stopped, and port inspectors get really worried when they see all this hardware. So my friend if you want to purchase weapons, then you have come to the right place."

That evening Olivier was sitting on his charter boat with the skipper and another man. Alex and Gerard had introduced him to the captain. He'd bought as much weaponry as he could afford and carry. He was well supplied with two pistols a light machine gun and a sniper rifle. The captain had supplied a motorised rubber skiff for him to use to get to the land. Alex had provided some night vision glasses as well as a couple of knives, water, and even some

American army rations.

Alex and Gerard had offered to pick up him and his wife with the ship. They would be leaving the port in 24 hours, they would stop the ship and wait for 12 hours just offshore at the far range of his rubber skiff. Olivier thanked them and gave each man a bear hug. With tears in his eyes, he'd boarded the yacht, and they'd set off for Somalia.

It was night when they'd arrived off the shore. The night was magnificently black, and Olivier could clearly see the milky way splashed across the sky. There were no lights on the shoreline, or at least any visible electrical lights although he did see some things which he thought might be fires. With the assistance of the captain and his crewman, Olivier inflated the skiff and got it over the side and loaded it with weapons and supplies. The sea was getting a little rough and the captain reminded him the forecast was for storms farther out to sea. It would make for rough sailing over the next 48 hours.

With a final handshake, Olivier climbed over the side and fired up the engine of the rubber skiff. Twisting the throttle, he moved the skiff away from the yacht and spun it round in a semi-circle. The skiff shot through the water as Olivier cranked up the throttle all the way. He wanted to get up some speed and then coast into the shore. The skiff took a pounding as it crashed from wave top to wave top. Olivier felt his teeth jarring as he made his way across the ocean towards the shore. Ahead of him he saw the shoreline tinted green by the night vision glasses.

Olivier turned the boat slightly to the right and let the engine die. He wanted to coast a little farther away from his engine noise. He scanned the shoreline closely. There was nobody on the beach. Olivier checked his equipment and looked for a place to come ashore. He picked up the oar and moved to the front of the skiff. He rowed into the shallow water and jumped out dragging the skiff onto the land. He removed the two air canisters from the skiff and set them aside.

Olivier depressed the value on the skiff, and the rubber began to deflate. As the boat deflated he dismounted the engine and carried it and the air canisters up the beach. Using the oar as a shovel, he dug a hole.

Returning to the now deflated skiff, he dragged it up the beach and wrapped the air canisters, and engine into the rubber and pushed everything into the hole and covered it with sand.

He buried the oar beside the hole and using the GPS marker on the satellite navigation system which Alex had supplied took the coordinates of the boat. He took a pen and paper out and scribbled down the location of the boat and memorised it as well, but he wouldn't depend on his memory.

The palest ink is better than the best memory.

Olivier smiled. It had been his drill instructor's favourite saying. He put the sat-nav round his wrist using the Velcro band and set the coordinates of the pirate camp. He took one last look round with the night-vision and then set off across the desert.

CHAPTER TWENTY

...

The four men gathered once more at the table inside the CIA headquarters in Paris. The last man to enter stood while the others opened notebooks and took out pens.

"We have a problem. It seems this French legionnaire has been allowed to escape." The man stopped momentarily and looked at one of the others for a long moment and then continued after the man nodded slightly. The two other men sensing a shift in the position of their comrade glanced at each other. They would soon be manoeuvring and jocking for his position.

"Regardless of this mistake, we have a situation where two of our agents have been killed by the local police. These men, we believe, are members of Les Retraités. We initially believed the legionnaire been taken away by Les Retraités, but it would seem they also don't know where he is. Our surveillance of Gregor Whitley and the Director General of DGSE has recorded a meeting where the two are discussing the disappearance of this man, and the death of one or possibly two of the French special forces sent to extract him."

One of the men raised a hand and the senior man nodded.

"Why do you say one or two?"

"Good question. Two bodies were found on a train in a compartment occupied by the fugitive," the man looked down and his notes and added. "Olivier Pinson. The French could identify one of the men, but not the other. It wasn't one of ours, or as far as we know, any of the other main players. I've got a team on that now."

"What about the third member of the in-country team?" the fourth man spoke for the first time. "He can identify this Olivier Pinson, who presumably is travelling under false papers now. Should we have him sent to Tanzania?"

"No, we've managed to get a copy of a

passport taken when Pinson travelled to the USA last year. I've distributed the picture to all operatives in North west Africa."

"If we're sure he doesn't have the memory stick or know it's location why pursue him?"

The senior man sighed, shook his head and glanced once more at the disgraced man.

"Just tying up loose ends. I also want to tie up another loose end. Our man in Somalia is becoming more of a hindrance than a help. I think it is time we put an end to this particular operation. I've discussed this with the director this morning, and he is going to have some military units engaged in peacekeeping take out this nest of extremists."

"And the French?"

"Fuck them. Emile has told the French they will kill the woman in three days. One of our informants in the French military has told us they are doing an insert and rescue in two days' time at midnight local time. The director will have our guys doing a search and destroy from six pm local time. We will have cleaned the area and hopefully taken control of the memory stick and extracted the woman before they arrive."

Gregor Whitley sat in his office with another man, a short stocky man with a scar across the bridge of his nose, looking at the map of Somalia and the surrounding area. The door buzzer rang, and Gregor opened it and followed in a heavyset man smoking a cigar. He introduced the man.

"Samuel Goldstein, this fat cigar smoking reprobate is the famous Carlos Sonatina."

Carlos moved his cigar to the other hand in order to shake Samuel's hand.

Gregor tapped the area on the map where Emile was camped. And all three crowed round the map.

"We know where Olivier is headed, but our man in the DGSE doesn't know how or when he is going to get there. There was one phone call where the DGSE man talked to Olivier and gave him the name and address of our man in Dar es Salaam. So either he has been picked up by the Cosa Nostra, the DGSE, the CIA, or this man Emile Duhon."

"Or he has decided to do something more lateral," said Samuel.

"Gregor," said Carlos, "This man Olivier isn't going to do anything predictable. He is a good soldier, and he knows surprise is his best weapon. He is maintaining radio silence. Olivier must know someone else in the area, or he is using the money the DGSE man gave him to good effect. I think we need to get some men down there to assess the situation and possibly help him."

"We can't. The director of the DGSE has issued instructions for us to turn him over to them, and he'll be watching us closely."

"I don't care," Carlos said. The cigar was being jabbed repeatedly back and forth as the man made his point. "We don't let our men down. We are back to first principles here. Les Retraités look out for the welfare of our brothers-in-arms. We've been looking out for our brothers and their families for one hundred and fifty years. I don't give a monkey's ass crack about the DGSE, Les Retraités look out for each other. We'll get some men down there and we help him get his wife back."

Gregor took a deep breath and then nodded.

"You are of course right. 'Les Retraités maintenir la fraternité.'"

All three men repeated together.

"Les Retraités maintenir la fraternité."

Gregor slapped his hand down on the table. "Right." He walked to the bar poured three glasses of whiskey. "We have some men down there now, a couple of members and some consultants. I think we could muster about ten men in a day or two."

"Get as many as you can, but make it one day. I doubt Olivier Pinson will give us time for protracted deployment," Carlos put the cigar back into his mouth as he spoke. "I will talk to our comrades in the Cosa Nostra. I don't want this man dead, I'll fix it."

The three men bent back over the map.

"I can fly down there," Gregor said. "I'll meet the men. We'll need a couple of helicopters."

"No, I'll go," said Samuel. "You're being followed by the CIA and the DGSE. Besides, I haven't seen Olivier since I trained him in hand-to-hand."

"If you want, then I'll get you on the private jet in an hour." Gregor said. "Hopefully, he'll recognise you."

"I hope so too, because I don't want to be on the wrong end of an angry Olivier Pison."

CHAPTER TWENTY-ONE

...

Olivier stopped a kilometre away from the coordinates of the encampment. Round him the ground was covered with scrub brush and some tough long bladed grass. He took out a knife, and cut a number of twigs and grass. He'd purchased a blanket while in the Tanzania. He began to stab the twigs into the blanket and wove the grass blades into the loose weave. He wanted to break up his outline and sneak towards the encampment. It was still daylight, and he wanted to reconnoitre the area before darkness. Olivier threw the blanket over his shoulders and walked closer to the encampment before crouching down and finally crawling as he came closer.

He heard the sound of motors in front of him as well as the laughter and speech of men. He was approaching the camp from the south where a road slithered across the desert. He paused, then began to move north-east where there was a small mound of a hill.

More of a sand castle than a hill. He though ruefully. *But hopefully it will be high enough.*

It took him almost an hour to make his way undetected, under the blanket of twigs, to the top of the mount. Olivier carefully took the sniper rifle from his back and positioned it on the ground. Reaching forward he pulled the two legs of the barrel tripod out. He lifted the scope covers up, and blew lightly on the lens to clear the fine shine of dust which had accumulated on them.

He scanned the entire encampment slowly with the sniper scope. There were twenty-eight men in the encampment, moving between the lorries and the tents. Only two permanent buildings were there, a large grey warehouse or barn, and a small house. There were two men on each wall standing guard over the house.

Curious, he thought, *why guard the house?*

Is that where they keep the hostages?

Ignoring this little puzzle for the moment Olivier looked over the remainder of the encampment looking for a clue to the location of his wife. The obvious place to keep the hostages was the warehouse, but it wasn't being guarded. Olivier closed the cap on the scope lenses. He rolled his body left and right slowly, creating an indentation in the sand for his body. He was going to be here for a while. It was another four hours until darkness.

He rested his head on his hands and watched the camp. The men were doing some training, mostly hand-to-hand and some others were doing some maintenance on the vehicles. Across the camp on the other side was a much higher hill. He froze as he saw a glint of light. The sun was high in the sky, but moving into the evening arc and its light had fallen on some kind of glass.

Lifting the caps on his scope, he moved with the speed of a glacier and eventually moved the rifle into a position to observe the other hillside. There were two men laying on the top of the hill. He could only just make out the top of their heads. Both of the men were holding a binoculars and scanning the encampment. Something was odd about them, which he couldn't quite place at first. Then he realised the two men were Caucasian. All the men in the camp were either African or Arabic in appearance.

They are going to attack, he thought. *I don't know who they are, but they don't match up with the men in the camp. I haven't seen any Caucasian not even my brother.*

He watched the two men as they slid away from the top of the hill and disappeared.

Why wouldn't Enrico, he corrected himself. *Why wouldn't Emile have men patrolling the outside of the camp? Where are the guards? Unless this is a trap? He's had years of military training, and he has never been incautious. Something is wrong here.*

Olivier used the sniper rifle to scan the area round the camp but didn't see anything. He turned slowly and used the scope to scan the area behind him. As he looked behind him, he saw two men hiding in a foxhole.

Merde! I've crawled into a trap. Emile has put some men in the camp as bait, and surrounded it with the rest of his men.

Olivier almost laughed out loud, but just grinned.

I don't want to be here when the trap springs, but I need to know where they are keeping Marie. He looked at the two men in the foxhole with grim determination. *Someone knows and if I took one of them I could force them to tell me.*

He considered this option while looking at the two men in the fox hole. It wasn't really an option, since they would be missed.

It doesn't really matter about this trap, she isn't going to be here. Emilie wouldn't put her as bait, unless he has this memory stick already.

Olivier sighed, then began to crawl down the hill and away from the encampment towards the foxhole. He needed information.

Olivier stopped about two metres from the men and the foxhole. They sat in the foxhole smoking and having a murmured conversation in Arabic. He reached behind his back slowly and pulled out the long combat knife. He didn't know how many fox holes were round, and he wasn't sure if he'd been heard.

This is a really bad idea. Really bad. But what else can I do?

Suddenly one of the men crushed out his cigarette and then lifted a military walkie-talkie. Olivier heard a something which he recognised as orders coming through the walkie-talkie. It didn't matter what the language, you could always tell when someone was giving orders.

Both of the men stood slowly and climbed out of the foxhole and crouched down they made their way away from the foxhole and away from Olivier position. He curses to himself, then stood into a crouch himself and followed the men. They moved away from the foxhole and towards a jeep which had been hidden under a pile of scrub brush. The two men quickly moved the brush out of the way and jumped into the jeep.

They drove off to the Northeast and Olivier stood perplexed.

They've obviously been called back, but to where?

He looked round him and a few dozen metres away he could see another jeep which was hidden from aerial view with scrub brush. It only took him a second to make a decision. He quickly and quietly moved down to the jeep and seeing the keys in the ignition he pulled the brush out of the seat and looked round one last time. There wasn't anyone nearby, he figured they would be in a foxhole somewhere round here too. Slipping into the seat of the jeep he started it. It fired up immediately, and he punched the petal and the vehicle jumped forward.

Olivier shot off across the desert, the scrub brush falling out of the jeep as he drove. In the rear-view he could see a couple men running out of the scrub with guns, but they didn't fire. Ahead of him were the two men who'd received orders. He followed them. He tried to remember if the men had taken the radio, but although he wasn't certain he didn't believe so.

Hopefully they'll not know who is following them, or if that this jeep is stolen. Lead on boys, lead on.

Olivier stopped the jeep after it clattered over another wooden bridge. Ahead of him the two men had entered a village and stopped. He watched them get out of the jeep and enter one of the shacks. He turned the jeep round and drove back down the road a little way. He stopped and quickly looked round the jeep. Olivier found a toolbox and opened it. Inside he took out the hammer and then used one of the pieces of scrub brush cuttings to wedge the steering wheel straight. He placed the hammer on the accelerator and the jeep began to move off across the desert. He watched it for a moment slowly picking up speed, and then he ran off in the opposite direction. He still had about two hours before darkness, and he wanted to recon the village.

Olivier took his time and circled round the village, he saw two men, possibly the same two emerge from a shack and jump back into the jeep. They spun out as they rushed back down the road in the direction of the trap at the encampment.

Olivier stopped and lay down on the highest ground he could find with the blanket draped over his back. He carefully took out the sniper rifle and scanned the village. He quickly determined all the villager's had been forced into a single shack the furthest away from the road which transected the village.

He used the rifle to check each and every shack in the small village. There were seven shacks in total, most of them corrugated iron sheets nailed on to wooden poles. On the opposite end of the village from the trapped villagers were a couple of men with rifles. These men stood just inside of the door of the shack and looking out. The shack where the two men from the jeep had entered had a radio mast stuck out the side of the ram-shackled wall.

Another building which was used as a barn for cattle had a vehicle hidden inside of it. The shack with the two men standing in the door seemed the most likely place for any captives. He decided to check there first.

Olivier scanned the area for guards or patrols but there was nothing. He slowly made his way as close to the shack as he dared in the daylight and then burrowed himself down into the dirt under the blanket and waited for darkness.

When the light had faded enough to make him an indistinct blur, he began to move up and against the wall of the shack. He crawled up to one of the holes in the corrugated iron walls and peered inside.

Two men stood guard inside of the shack. Marie was sat on a box with her hands and feet tied. The two men both had rifles, but no side-arms. They were taking turns looking out the door, which they left open in order to look out of. Olivier crawled round to the side of the shack and looked out over the village to see who might be watching the shack. The other shack with the radio mast standing out of it was off to his right, and they wouldn't have a clear view of this shack. Directly across the dirt road from this shack was the barn which held the vehicle.

Best to take care of these two and then melt into the desert, but I don't know when they were last relieved. Can't really take a chance on the vehicle, I don't know if it will start.

Olivier stood and took a deep breath. He reached into his jacket and from an underarm holster pulled the silenced pistol. He walked round the corner of the shack and strode up to the door. He walked inside and fired twice into the face of the man at the door. Thud, thud. Olivier turned to his right slightly and brought the pistol round. The second guard was trying to stand when two rounds caught him in the head. The body fell backward. Marie stood silently staring at him. To give her credit, she didn't make a sound, but he brought his finger to his lips anyway.

Olivier pulled out a knife with his left hand and cut her restraints holding the pistol in his right hand.

"Oh god, Olivier," she said. "Oh god."

Olivier grabbed her and held her close for a moment. They stood silently holding each other for a few moments until finally he pushed her slightly away and put the knife back into his belt.

"When will they change guards?" he whispered.

"They don't. These two have been here yesterday and today." She replied. Her face was stained with tears. "I can't believe you are here. I never thought…"

He put a finger against her lips, then kissed her.

"You're a spy?" he said softly into her ear.

"Oh, didn't I mention that?" she whispered, "I must have forgotten."

CHAPTER TWENTY-TWO

...

Emile flipped the assault rifle back over his shoulder and picked up the small radio which his man held out to him.

"Two sniper teams located on reference points six and thirteen."

"As soon as you hear gunshots, or explosions, kill them if I haven't already called you." Emile calmly gave the orders in a low tone.

His patrols had spotted the Americans moving forward into the encampment, but they had been warned the day before by villagers who'd heard the helicopters dropping them off. His men's orders were to charge the encampment as soon as they heard gunshots or flash-bangs. The men inside of the encampment were all entrenched in the warehouse and the small house. The walls of both buildings had been reinforced and all best sniper positions within a mile had been determined and a four of his own snipers were covering those spots with a L115A3 British Army sniper rifle who's effective range was 2.5 kilometres and equipped with night vision scopes. Unbeknown to both Emile and Olivier, Emile's snipers had got into position and had only missed seeing Olivier on the small mount by a few minutes.

Emile had eight men with SA-24 Grinch 9K338 Igla-S portable air defence missiles standing by to shoot down any rescue helicopters or attack helicopters the Americans might deploy. The SA-24's could also be used for aircraft, but he was hoping they wouldn't use stealth fighters.

They are after the woman and the memory stick, they're not going to blow everything up, they're depending on the special forces to retrieve it, and they think they are up against untrained, poorly armed militants.

Emile grinned, these men weren't militants, they were a military. They were the core of the army he was going to use to take over enough land to create his own country, and with the backing of the Russians for arms and equipment he would change the face of Africa.

Wham!

Bright lights appeared on the horizon where Emile was standing. The assault on the encampment had begun. Still holding the radio in his hand he ordered the deaths of the two snipers. The men round him were racing forward into the encampment. Emile paused and tapped the SA-24 operator on the head and pointed his two fingers to his eyes. The man nodded and turned his eyes to the sky.

Ahead Emile's men had already made it to the firing position which had been selected for them over the encampment. Below he could see a knot of soldiers trying to retreat as they came under fire from all directions. They were retreating in this direction. Emile's men knelt down and waited without firing.

Two quotes from Sun Tzu and the art of war had influenced his strategy for this evening. 'To a surrounded enemy, you must leave a way of escape' and 'Show him there is a road to safety, and so create in his mind the idea that there is an alternative to death. Then strike.'

Emile had purposefully encouraged the trapped soldiers to travel in this direction. Moving north and into the small brush covered hillock where his men now knelt, assault rifles and machine guns ready to fire. His men were arranged in a V-shape with himself and four others at the bottom of the V, arranged, so they wouldn't be cross-firing into each other. The Americans were moving swiftly in his direction. He could see them clearly through the night vision goggles, shifting back and forth in two well-formed and discipled groups. They were giving covering fire back towards the encampment as they retreated.

Overhead Emile heard the sounds of helicopters and then the scream of rockets as his SA-24 operators fired. Above him and to the left a huge explosion as a helicopter was blown out of the sky. The encampment was flooded with bright light and then a second explosion followed shortly after. Two helicopters down.

Emile watched the surviving ground troops and waited until they were into the V-shape of his men's formation. Emile stood and opened fire, and all of his men stood and followed suit. The Americans were torn to pieces as gunfire raked them from two sides.

Emile and his men continued to fire constantly until every one of the special forces were laying motionless on the ground. He threw his assault rifle to his lieutenant.

"Search them for ID, and make sure they are all dead. Take pictures of the faces. I'm going back to the village. I'm going to talk to this woman again."

He held up a combat knife and the lieutenant nodded.

"I'm sure she'll tell you what you want to know."

I've completely ruined their plans, time to up the stakes, Emile thought. He reached into his pocket and flipped open his phone, speed dialling a French number.

"Go ahead and launch," he said when the phone was answered without preamble. "Call me back when it is done."

Driving down the dark desert road Emile smiled to himself, in two hours time a mortar attack would destroy the CIA's secret Paris office. Things did seem to be going his way.

I just need to find this memory stick, such a pity my poor brother is to become a widower.

His laughter rang out across the desert night, the cool wind blowing the oceans salt air inland. Ahead of him he could see some dim lights from the village and pulled up to the shack where the woman was being held. He stopped the jeep and leaped out. Something made the skin crawl on his arms, and Emile swung the assault rifle round off his back and pointed it at the door of the shack. He approached cautiously. One of his men should have reacted by now.

He ran to the side of the shack and put his back against the wall and carefully peered round the corner. Inside by the light of a small gas lantern he could see the dead bodies of two of his men and the cut ropes.

Merde, merde, merde!

He moved away and silently approached the shack with the radio operator and guards. He kicked the flimsy door in and saw four men leaping for their rifles.

"Stop!" he waved them back down, lowering his rifle. "The woman has escaped and the guards are dead! Get the jeep ready and go down to the river. She will probably try that way again."

Suddenly the radio burst into life and the radio operator looked up at Emile.

"The encampment is under attack again. Our men have been caught off guard," he paused for a moment and listened on his headphones. "The lieutenant thinks it is the French, he's heard French voices, and they are using H&K416 assault rifles."

"Merde! Well, there isn't anything we can do to help them now. We need to find the woman," he stopped and pointed at the men giving orders rapid-fire. Each of the men left the shack and Emile collected up two other men one who was guarding the other jeep and one who was watching the villagers. He had six men in total who all gathered outside in front of the two now running jeeps.

"You three," he pointed at the radio operator and two others, "get into that jeep and get down to the intersection of the ravine and the river. Wait there, but spread out. Use the night vision goggles and watch for the woman."

Emile turned to the remaining men.

"You're with me, we'll start by searching

here for tracks, get the lights out of the jeeps and turn that jeep round to shine the headlamps. Try to find tracks for the woman, and whoever helped her to escape. I want to know how many of them and what direction they are going. Now let's move!"

"Looks like only one man and the woman," the man said turning to Emile. "They started off moving south, but they've since curved round and are heading east towards river."

Emile nodded. "They are heading for the river, the woman must have hidden the memory stick there. Let's go!" He gestured for the two men to lead.

My brother, without a doubt. He's brought the entire French army with him to rescue his wife. But it doesn't matter, I'm going to have that memory stick. He is a slippery little shit, Emile couldn't help but feel some admiration for his little brother's tenacity. *He doesn't give up. Should I warn these two? He might have left behind anti-personnel mines, or be waiting with a sniper rifle. Oh well.*

They were moving swiftly running along the ground, the point man holding an electrical lamp pointed at the ground and tracking the occasional scuff mark or foot print. Night vision wasn't any good for tracking. Emile was watching the tracker when suddenly the entire back of his head exploded in a red mist and the lantern went arcing through the air.

"Take cover!" Emile shouted as he threw himself on the ground rolling. He kept rolled away towards some rocks as another shot pinged off the ground beside him. He rolled into a ball behind the small rock trying to reduce the target space. He looked up slowly taking in the surrounding area with his night vision glasses.

"Sniper," the other man said.

"Aren't you the king of the fucking obvious." Emile said.

There was no telling where the shot came from other than it was forward of their current position. They couldn't stay here pinned down, but his brother couldn't continue to wait forever either. The sniper shot was a delaying tactic, he wouldn't wait.

"Come on, let's go. We know they are heading for the river, so when I go, break for the ravine, and we'll move down there towards the river."

Emile stood up and began to run in a zigzag pattern towards the ravine. He didn't wait or look back to see if the other man was following. He jumped down into the ravine and then turned putting his back against the far side. A few seconds later his man jumped over the edge following him.

"It will take us longer following the ravine, but the other men are already waiting, so we just need to herd them towards the river."

CHAPTER TWENTY-THREE

...

"I've killed one of them," Olivier said to her. "There are two more following, but they are staying down for the moment. We should be going towards the ocean."

"I have to recover the memory stick," she said. He was clicking the arms back against the sniper rifle and slinging it over his back. "I have to."

"Fine," he said abruptly, "but we need to move now."

"I was in this ravine when I escaped before, if we follow it then it will lead to a river and a grove of trees where I hid the memory stick."

Olivier pointed up at the sky. The soft light of the moon was coming through the clouds and becoming stronger.

"We don't want to be running in the open. Hold my hand and stay behind me. I can see better with the goggles. We'll grab this memory stick and use the river to get south to the beach. I've got a boat stowed and a ship waiting for us."

Marie stopped him and leaned against him, she kissed him passionately before they broke and began to run down the ravine.

"I can see the river," Olivier said, putting his arm back to stop her. He took the sniper rifle off his back and used the night-scope to scan the area. Suddenly the sound of a heavy calibre weapon sounded in the night and the lip of the ravine was shredded by bullets.

Olivier yanked her towards the ground and lay on top of her as the fifty calibre rounds were ripping the ground above them and ricocheting off the rocks nearby. The shooting stopped as quickly as it had begun.

"Crawl! Crawl!" he shouted at her. He rolled off her and pushed her further down the ravine. He stood quickly and snapped off two shots towards the direction of the machine gun. Other smaller arms opened up, and he lay the rifle barrel down against the edge of the ravine and located the jeep. On the back of it was mounted a fifty calibre, with someone desperately trying to clear a jam. Olivier took a quick breath and let it out smoothly as he curled his finger on the trigger. The machine gunner flew backward off the jeep. Small arms firing on Olivier's position started up, ducking back down into the ravine, he crouched and ran down a few meters. Marie had stopped and was holding her rifle against her chest. She looked at him, Olivier watched her take a deep breath and then stood up pointing the rifle over the edge of the ravine and firing.

Olivier pulled the trigger twice taking down another man. The sniper rifle was out of ammunition and Olivier threw it to the ground swinging his assault rifle up and firing at the jeep. Marie stopped firing and was ducked down beside Olivier's leg reloading her rifle.

"Behind!" she shouted.

Olivier spun round and fired into the chest of the man who was running up the ravine. Behind him he could see his brother dropping to the ground and taking cover behind the body.

"Up and over!" Olivier grabbed her arm, and they jumped up over the edge of the ravine and rolling away.

"Stephano, brother! Give me the memory stick and I'll let you and your wife go!"

Olivier rolled on his side and levelled his rifle. Under the jeep he could see the legs of two men. He opened fire. Screams sounded from the jeep and Olivier killed the two men as they fell.

"Run for the jeep, we have to get out of here."

"What about the memory stick?" she said taking a hold of his arm.

"Damn the memory stick! We have to get out of here!"

"No," she ran towards a grove of trees and Olivier had no choice but to follow her.

Olivier ran behind her into the small grove of trees. *Nobody following*. Olivier looked round keeping his gun up and ready.

"Hurry!"

Behind him he heard Marie scrambling round from tree to tree. Olivier watched the ravine carefully, the green glow of the night vision allowing him to check the area. He saw Emile jump out of the ravine and run for the jeep. Firing off a couple of shots he moved forward but the shots missed his brother.

"You need to hurry up," Olivier fired again at the jeep, on the top of the jeep was a radio under the fifty calibre. "He is trying to call in reinforcements."

"I can't find it."

Olivier took a careful aim and fired three shots into the back of the jeep. One of the shots hit the radio which fell over, out of sight. Emile's arm darted over the edge of the jeep and dragged the radio over the side. Olivier fires a couple more rounds into the radio before it disappears over the edge of the jeep.

"I think I hit the radio, but we really need to get moving."

"I found it." Marie touched his shoulder. "We can go."

"I have called in more men!" Emile's voice floated up from behind the jeep and Olivier turned to Marie and points towards the river.

"Crawl down to the river and start swimming. I'll hold him here for a few minutes and then join you."

Olivier sighed with relief when she didn't argue with him but started to crawl down the river.

"We'll swap you, the memory stick for the jeep!" Olivier shouted. He shifted his position, moving towards his left, but keeping the rifle pointed at the jeep. No answer from the jeep and Olivier tried to find his brother. To his right Marie was almost at the river.

"Do you hear? We'll swap the memory stick for the jeep!"

Where is he? Olivier thought and began to crawl forward towards the jeep when Marie screamed.

Olivier turned and then stood slowly. His brother stood beside the river with a pistol to Marie's head. She had dropped her gun, but still had the memory stick in her hand.

"Give me the memory stick." Emile told her, never taking his eyes off his brother and the rifle. "Give it to me, and we'll all just go our separate ways."

Olivier began to walk towards him, the rifle never wavering as he aimed.

"Marie," Olivier said as he walked towards them. "I want you to throw the memory stick as hard as you can into the river."

"No!" both Marie and Emile said at the same time.

"I want you to throw the memory stick into the water."

"I'll kill her little brother."

"Then I'll kill you. Only, I'll kill you really fucking slow."

Olivier continued to walk towards them, his gun never moving away from the forehead of his brother.

"You will not let her die. Just give me the memory stick!" Emile shouted this last into her ear and jerked her head sideways.

Olivier stood looking at them, behind him he heard the sound of helicopters. He allowed his rifle barrel to lower slightly. Marie looked at him, staring into his eyes. His brother started to smile.

"Let her go." Olivier said.

"No." Emile said. As his finger began to curl on the trigger Marie swung round twisting away and dropping to the ground.

Without her Emile had no shield and both men knew it. Olivier was lifting the rifle barrel at the same time as Emile tried to bring his pistol round towards Olivier.

Three shots rang out. Olivier watched as

the burst took his brother in the chest. Emile fell back into the river, his lifeless fingers dropping the pistol and blood pouring from his chest.

"Let's go!" Olivier shouted at Marie, and they ran for the jeep as the sound of helicopters grew loud in the sky.

CHAPTER TWENTY-FOUR

...

Three days later in a restaurant on the Champs-Elysees in Paris, Olivier and Marie sat sipping wine and speaking with Cyrille.

"The director wants to talk to you," Cyrille told Marie. "I don't think he is very happy."

"Speak of the devil." Marie said, pointing at the door where the Director of the DGSE was walking into the restaurant, followed by Gregor Whitley.

"Do you have it?" the director said to Marie.

"Bonjour," she said her voice dripping with sarcasm. "I'm glad you're here, I want to tender my resignation."

Gregor smiled at the exchange and waved his hand at a chair and Olivier nodded. Gregor sat down at the table and leaned close to Olivier. "I have a job for you."

"I'm retired." Olivier said.

"Of course, We all are." Gregor said, and waved for the waitress.

"I want that memory stick!" the director shouted and a number of people turned their heads to look. Marie reached into her bag and took out the memory stick and handed it to him.

The director looked relieved, then looked

at Marie.

"Your resignation isn't accepted. Both of you in my office tomorrow at nine." The director pointed at both Cyrille and Marie. He turned and walked out the door of the restaurant.

Gregor laughed and ordered a bottle of champagne.

"Don't worry, the director will be out of a job soon. He is under investigation for ordering operations without official sanction. There has also been an unexplained explosion in Paris laid at his door by the Americans. I doubt that recovery of the memory stick will help him much, but he seems to have pinned his hopes on it."

The waitress brought the champagne and Gregor opened it and toasted them all for their safe return.

"I have a job opening with Les Retraités for both you and Marie if your interested?"

Olivier looked at Marie, and they stood up together.

"We'll think about it, but right now we're going home." Olivier shook their hands, and Marie gave Cyrille a kiss on the cheek. As they walked out of the restaurant, Gregor looked at Cyrille.

"You owe me a favour," Gregor said. Cyrille looked nervous and Gregor continued. "But all I want in return is for you to convince them to work for me."

"I'm sure that will not be a problem."

CHAPTER TWENTY-FIVE

Excerpt from "Italian Détente - book two of "Les Retraités

Olivier ran down the forest path, dodging right and left as bullets thudded into the surrounding trees. Behind him the two Mafia gunmen ran, panting and gasping as they chased him.

Olivier looked round at the woodlands and made a snap decision to stay on the path. The men behind him weren't in shape. The oldest one was losing ground rapidly, and the younger one wasn't much better. Olivier had only been out of the Foreign Legion for a year, and he'd maintained his fitness regime. The path was arching up into a sharp incline.

The hill will slow them down more. He

scanned the area. *I need a weapon.*

Another bullet whizzed past his head making him duck. The ground was muddy from recent rains and running up the slippery hill was hard going. The path, covered in bicycle tracks where cyclists had churned the ground, was a muddy bog.

Suddenly his foot slipped, and Olivier tumbled to the ground. A bullet took a huge chunk of bark out of the tree in front of him.

The fall that saved your life, he thought. He scrambled to stand, beside him on the ground was a stick about the size of his thumb and as long as his forearm. Olivier snatched up the stick and continued to run up the hill, trying to keep trees between him and the two men behind. As he topped the hill, glancing behind, he saw the young man was about halfway up the hill but the older man had stopped. The old man leaned against a tree panting and holding his chest. Olivier grinned running downhill now, it would be easier.

Ahead in the path, Olivier saw a mud hole and threw himself into a forward roll. He tucked in his head and landed on his left shoulder, rolling onto his back and then back to his feet in a single move. His body dripped with messy, sticky mud and as he ran he slapped the mud on his face and massaged it into his hands covering his skin.

Glancing back, he saw the top of the young guy's head topping the hill.

Gotta hide.

Olivier lay down behind a tree in a small pile of leaves. Grabbing up leaves with his left hand he pulled them over his body. The camouflage wasn't great but with the mud and the leaves stuck to him he hoped the man wouldn't see him.

He was hidden behind a tree which would be on the mobsters right. Olivier laid on his back with his right hand extended out over his head, the long stick held tightly in his hand. He waited until the young mobster ran round the tree and Olivier sat up sharply driving the stick straight into the man's groin.

The man screamed as the stick penetrated his intestines. Olivier yanked the stick out as he stood. He rammed the bloody stick into the man's eye, holding the body as it slumped, trying to grab the gun.

A shout from the top of the hill and the crack of a pistol, as the gun dropped from the dead man's hands and into the leaves.

Olivier dropped the body and abandoned the search for the gun. Running, shifting right and left he ran as fast as he could.

I can outrun this fat fucker, he thought, then felt the hot white heat and pain of a bullet slamming into his left arm.

"Merde!" he cried out, his body spinning round from the impact of the bullet and knocking him to his knees. He launched himself forward and started run again down the hill.

At the bottom of the hill the path split. He could see one path lead up to a small road and some kind of wooden fence. The other path split left and moved deeper into the woods and away from the road. The left path would lead him over the mountain and towards the sea. On the road, at the top of the right path, he saw a lorry filled with men.

Merde, more of them. Decision made for me.

Olivier took the left path as another shot rang out and the men in the lorry cut loose with an assortment of weapons. Olivier felt his lungs burning, and he gasped for breath. He'd not run this hard for a long time, but he was pulling away. Suddenly, in front of him, the path turned sharply and went left again following a large chain-link fence. The fence was long, about waist high. Behind him weapons fire was cutting down branches and ricocheting off the wood. Olivier didn't stop or slow down as he approached the chain link fence and simply leaped over it as he ran.

Less than a meter the other side of the fence, the ground ended in a concrete edge. Olivier stumbled and fell headlong over the edge of the precipice his arms flailing.

CHAPTER TWENTY-SIX
OTHER BOOKS YOU MAY ENJOY

A LETTER FROM THE AUTHOR

Hello Dear Reader,

Thanks for reading my book. I really appreciate your time and I hope you enjoyed the book. I wanted to let you know can always get up to date list of titles, free e-books, free extracts, and the possibility to become a beta-reader for new fiction books, when you sign up for our fiction newsletter.

Share it! If you liked this book please lend it to a friend who may like it. If you can't share it, then please spread the word. Most books are purchased because of recommendations, and I'd love for you to recommend this book.

Review it! Please consider posting a short review where you purchased the book. Honest reader reviews help others decide if they'll enjoy a book.

Connect with me and check out my website and blog.

Regards,
Rick Dearman

To get more information on upcoming titles, free e-books, free extracts, and the possibility to become a beta-reader for new fiction books, please sign up for our fiction newsletter.

Other books you may enjoy:

LES RETRAITÈS SERIES

Veterans of the French Foreign Legion are some of the hardest, toughest, and most ruthless individuals ever to have put on a uniform. The Legion's toughness and ruthlessness are indisputable and the Legion, this bleak, cruel fighting machine, is loyal only to its own. Every man who completes his time becomes eligible for French citizenship and receives a certificate declaring he has done his duty with "honneur et fidélité." On retirement from this brotherhood there is second brotherhood, a semi-secret society over 150 years old. The men who have retired from the legion, ex-legionaries, who have formed an elite secret society, a society who's only membership requirement is your certificate of honneur et fidélité. This society is Les

Retraités. If you need their help, you can ask for it, but Les Retraités always want a favour in return.

"African Extrication" book one of "Les Retraités"

Somalian pirates are going to learn a lesson about kidnapping the wife a Retraités. Olivier Pinson is going to save his wife and nothing is going to stop him. Not the African wilderness, the spies of the Générale de la Sécurité Extérieure and the CIA, not the Cosa Nostra, nor his own brother. Olivier is a man on a mission.

"Italian Détente" book two of "Les Retraités"

Another hard-hitting adventure in the Les Retraités series. Olivier Pinson tries to make peace, but war is easier for the ex-legionnaire.

THE FRONTIERSMAN SERIES

A gritty fusion of fantasy and western the Frontiersman series has as its setting the immense plains, rugged tablelands, and dizzying mountain ranges bordering three nations all striving to gain control. The Frontiersman is a story of one man's struggle to carve out a new life for himself in a land of brutal weather, savage people and fantastic beings. Follow the half-breed Cheveyo as he fights back against the savage climate and the even more savage inhabitants of the frontier.

"Wild Justice" book one of "Frontiersman" is available on Amazon or Kobo.

"A gripping story of blood, revenge, love and fighting for what you believe is right even if it isn't your fight..."

The civil war is over and the rebellion lost. Cheveyo the half-breed rebel is travelling to the frontier to start a new life with only two pure-bred horses and dreams of a ranch. But after happening on to the remains of a murdered family. He decides to give them the justice his family never got.

Using his skills and training to track down the killers and dispense justice he discovers these killers are just a few of the renegades working for the man they call "Big Red". Crossing "Big Red" could cost him his life. It will take all of his skills to remain alive and a man of principle in the hellish frontier.

"Indomitable" book two of "Frontiersman" is available on Amazon or Kobo.

"Fighting for your place could mean losing everything you love..."

Cheveyo is making a new life for himself in the mountains above Oxmead. Finally his dreams of a ranch and a home are starting to come true; but new arrivals and old enemies are making their way into the frontier and Cheveyo will have to confront his past and defend his future in the exciting new instalment of the action packed Frontiersman series.

"Blood Circle" book three of "The Frontiersman"

COMING SOON

Cheveyo emerges from the mountains with three goals on his mind. Capture the black stallion, kill the migrant priest who stole his ranch, and get his land back. But the frontier is engulfed in a war, the land is being raided by the followers of the Blood God, and the bear-men are murdering humans. What can one man do armed only with his hatchets and his skill against a world at war? Cheveyo will need all his wits and savage skills to survive in the exciting final instalment of the action packed Frontiersman series.

THE LIBRARIAN SERIES

"Ignition" book one of "The Librarian" available on Amazon or Kobo.

The City of Ettengard is under siege. The Library has been given an impossible mission, the Head Librarian and the Chief Mage have been poisoned. Ranperen and Tantia the young students must make their way across a war torn country to find a cure and to save the library from destruction. Inside the city the clashes between the thieves guild and the beggars are becoming bloodier as the war causes unrest and rebellion. And a mysterious group of conspirators are trying to bring back the glory days of the defeated and evil Empire.

"Combustion" book two of "The Librarian"

COMING SOON

"Inferno" book three of "The Librarian"

COMING SOON

TO BE THE FIRST TO KNOW ABOUT NEW RELEASES, OR EVEN BECOME A BETA-READER DON'T FOR GET TO SIGN UP TO OUR NEWSLETTER.

www.ingramcontent.com/pod-product-compliance
Lightning Source LLC
La Vergne TN
LVHW091257150826
845673LV00006B/1456